Audacity to Survive

Audacity to Survive

Beatrice Edwards Reeves

Library of Congress Control Number: 2010907299
ISBN: Hardcover 978-1-4535-0611-0
Softcover 978-1-4535-0610-3
Ebook 978-1-4535-0612-7

This book was printed in the United States of America.

To order additional copies of this book, contact:
Xlibris Corporation
1-888-795-4274
www.Xlibris.com
Orders@Xlibris.com
81048

This book is dedicated to my mother,
Mrs. Esther J. Edwards

CHAPTER ONE

It was in a scenic tiny fishing town on the northern shores of Canada, called Green Meadows, where this story takes place. It was a lovely, friendly town and was also a tourist attraction with its blue oceans and green lawn and meadows as far as the eye could see. Beth sat at her window and stared at the lovely surroundings of her yard and listened to the birds sing and the gurgling of the brook as she thought how things can change so quickly. She stared at the flowers that ran by her yard as the thoughts came running through her memory of a terrible and tragic time in her life. She was a strong, confident woman who survived many things in her life. This is her story.

On that particular morning, the birds were singing, and the sun shone on the ocean like sparkling diamonds. She smiled sadly and thought, *What a lovely life, if one had not had so much misery in it.* She put her gnarled hands together and, with tears in her now faded blue eyes, went back in reminiscing. The town supported itself by fishing and mining, to which many a poor miner died from a disease called black lung. And many a poor fisherman drowned, trying to make a living on these dangerous and rocky shores. Beth was one of fifteen in her large family. Her mother was a struggling housewife and her father a poor fisherman. They had to scramble day by day to make ends meet. Beth was the second eldest sister. She started at a young age, working to help the family survive as did her older brothers. In those days you were sent out to do odd jobs to help out. Her mother was a kind, loving woman who struggled to bring up her family as best she could while her father was a loud mouthed man who was strict on the children, especially at the dinner table. If they did not finish what was on their plate, they had to eat it for the morning meal. Many times Beth had to do this. One day something happened to her mother that changed Beth's outlook on life.

She had gone to the little store across the bridge. It was the only one they had in the town, so it was very busy at all times. Her mother had asked Beth to go with her to help bring home their month's supply of food, for back then they shopped once a month and had to buy everything, right down to a pencil. That day her mother was talking to Mrs. Lise, the store owner. Beth was looking around, not paying too much attention. All of a sudden, Mrs. Lise was talking very loudly to her mother. Beth went over and saw tears in her mother's eyes as the lady was saying, "I cannot let you have your month's supply of food, because you still owe me for last month." Beth eyes also filled with tears at the look on her mothers face as they left the store; she was only twelve years old, but she vowed that day that no matter what it took, her mother would never have to beg for food for her family again. In the years that went by, Beth kept that promise and worked at cleaning other people's homes, carried water to homes, scrubbed the church walls, and anything that she could do, for she did not want to see her mother cry. As the years went by, most of the older brothers and sisters moved. Her father took to bootlegging of the French shores, and he drank more than ever, to which he started abusing her mother. Many a night Beth would stay up with her mother to wait for him to come home from one of these "runs," as they called it. Her mother would turn off the lights and leave just the one light on in the hallway for it faced the ocean, and when he got close into the harbor to dock, the light was a signal that it was safe to come ashore.

He sold a lot of it and made a living when he was not fishing. But he also drank a lot. It became a way of life; the children learned early that you had to do anything to survive, and it became commonplace to hear the children say, "My dad is a bootlegger," for there were many families doing the same thing. But his drinking got worse, and his abuse on her mother increased. It got to the point that when they heard him coming back from the local bar, they would grab their mother and go out the back door while the others hid under their beds, or climbed out the windows in terror of this man. One night in particular, Beth remembered, they heard him cursing on their mother through the open window as he came up the drive. Beth grabbed her mother's arm and had to pull her out the door; it was very late at night. They ran around the back of the house and ran to Aunt Lena next door. She knew what Toni was like, for she heard him pass by her home many a night, ranting against his family. She saw Beth and her mother come to the door, quickly, and quietly she ushered them inside, and they hid in her closet. Their hearts were beating so fast out of fear of this monster of a man. It seemed like hours went by before Beth calmed down. Then suddenly they heard a sound. They froze, for it was a door opening. Aunt Lena must have forgotten to lock it. Beth was so terrified that she held her breath as did her mother. The silence was deafening; it was like he was listening for them to breathe.

Suddenly, Aunt Lena said, "Toni, how did you get in here? You have to leave now and go home to get some sleep." "I'm looking for Essie," he replied. "Have you seen her?"

"Of course not, Toni. I haven't seen her in a while. Tell her to come visit, trying to sound casual. Good night now, Toni. I must lock up, it's late."

Beth had tears in her eyes and waited for him to leave, all the while praying that he would not hurt Mrs. Lena. She was a big woman but was also sick. He finally left, cursing on her mother and saying that when he found her, she would be sorry. It was a long time before Beth and her mother came out of that closet. Mrs. Lena finally coaxed them out at about dawn, assuring them that the doors were now locked, and that she had watched Toni go home. When they thought it was safe and figured that he was asleep, they quietly walked toward the house and went in to get some sleep.

That was the way their lives went until Beth could not take it anymore. Someone had to stand up to this man. It was a miserable life, and it got worse as the years went by. Beth started standing up to her father now more and more every day. She now ran the household as her mother was beaten down by this man, so much so that Beth had enough. So it came to a head when he came home like a raving maniac one day. Beth was ready for him. He came in the door with a piece of board to hit her mother. Her brother Harry, who had come home the night before and had been filled in on what was transpiring all this time, had a rifle pointed in his direction. "You bastard, if you raise your hand to hit my mother, I'll blow your legs off."

The look on her father's face was something to see. He leaned against the wall unsteadily and sneered, "You go straight to hell. You were never around, why come back now? You are no good, to have walked out on your own family years ago. You are no son of mine."

"Well," Harry spat out, "look who I learned it from. A good-for-nothing drunk."

With that, the old man, as we called him now, staggered into the hallway, dropping the board along the way. "To hell with the lot of you," he snarled.

Life went on like that for many years. Her father did not abuse her mother as much now since Harry had the confrontation with him. Her brother stayed around for a few months, then was gone on his way again. Beth stayed close to her mother through these years. After a few months, he was on his rampage again. He came home one night and cleaned the house out, threw everything out the windows. Beth thought this was the very worst that she had seen him. The next morning he got up from sleeping it off and asked what happened, as he always did. This was too much for Beth. She snapped, and everything that they had endured at the hands of this man came out. She told him off so fiercely that her mother was fearful that he was going to really hurt Beth. But she kept going until she was done. She calmed down after her mother had to slap her.

She looked him straight in the eye. "You will not touch my mother again or destroy everything in this house, for if you do, as God is my witness, I will take that rifle and blow your brains out all over this kitchen." Her voice had gone low and quiet in tone, and her father stared. And he knew that this woman, his daughter, would do as she said. There was a heavy silence; Beth was terrified now and very pale and shaking, as she stood her ground. She held his stare; her father stood up all of a sudden and towered over them both.

Her mother shrank faintly against a chair. He said in a loud voice, "You are no longer a daughter of mine. And you can get the hell out of my house."

Beth got very angry. "As long as my mother is in this house, then so will I, for I'm not going anywhere." She raised her voice. "And I'm going to be watching you every moment. If you get liquored up, go sleep in the barn," she screamed in his face.

She, all of a sudden, took the rifle off the wall and said, "To protect my mother and family that you have not driven away yet, I'm willing to go to jail to protect them, and by God I will."

The old man stared at this young woman. He suddenly realized that she was the only one besides his son that had stood up to him, but he still did not like her, for his children were like strangers to him as he never had any time for them. Beth walked toward her mother after putting the rifle back on the wall. It was her dad's hunting rifle back in happier days. He used to take his sons on moose hunting trips. They would come home after a week's hunting with enough meat to feed the neighborhood. Tears welled in Beth's eyes now as she thought of those happy times. They were very, very poor back then but were happy. On legs that felt like Jelly, Beth sank into a chair. Her mother was quietly weeping in a corner. She went to her and said, "Mother, someone had to do this, if not it will continue."

But her mother knew her husband. He was not finished, and that worried her, for he was capable of hurting his own child, as he was like this when they first married. There seemed to be a little difference in the home now as Beth was watching him all the time when he went on binges. She now locked him outside to rant and rave. He soon learned that this family had enough of this life, and he slowly calmed down. But it was not all because of Beth's actions; his health was declining. In the days that followed, he was really getting sick. He still had a few binges, but not bad ones.

One evening Beth went to a movie with her friends at the urging of one of her sisters and her mother. It was a sober night as the old man was home sleeping and not feeling too good. He had been to the doctor that week and was having stomach problems and headaches. Beth figured, as they all knew, that it was from the many years of heavy work and drinking. That night she went and had a really good time. Some of her friends called her an old maid Jokingly that night for not marrying, as yet. She laughed. "My day will come."

As she told her mother and sister Meg that she would be home by eleven, she hurried home. She was thinking about the changes that had come to the home now as she walked up the drive to her house. The lights were off, she walked in the door. "That's strange," she thought. The lights were never off until late, especially tonight as Meg had said that she would be up waiting for her as she wanted to know all the details of her night out. She left the lights off.

"Oh, well." She smiled. "I'll tell her all about it tomorrow." She liked this solitude, she thought. She went and sat by the window, looking out at the misty night, for it had become misty and foggy when she walked home. The weather changed almost every hour here in these parts of the North. Suddenly she heard a slight noise.

"Is that you, Meg?" she asked. As she looked closer, her blood ran cold, for not two feet away stood her father. He had been drinking, for now she could tell, he staggered a little. The light from the hall made him look like a demonic being of some sort.

"You are late," he snarled quietly.

Beth summoned her courage. "I'm not late," she replied. "I'm an adult, I come and go as I please."

She watched as her father, a little unsteady, came toward her. She looked in horror as he held the rifle in his hand and was pointing it to her face. Pushing the gun into her head, he said, "I should blow your head off."

Beth's heart was beating so fast that she was sure he could hear it. She summoned up all her courage and replied, "Go ahead. Do what you think you have to do." Her legs turned to rubber as she now struggled to stand and face him. He stared into her face for a long time, searching for the fear that was bubbling up inside her. Beth stood rooted to the spot. Then he lowered the rifle slightly and said, "You are not worth it." Having said that in a savage tone, he slammed out the door. Beth sank into the chair, sobbing so loudly that her mother and Meg ran out to the kitchen.

Meg noticed the bruise where he had roughly stuck the gun to her head. "You have to leave here, Beth." She was ringing her hands and crying, as was her mother. "Yes, you leave for a few days," she said, "Harry will be here tomorrow night. We will be allright."

Meg sobbed, "He has been talking about hurting you all night. I didn't know where you would be after the movie to warn you not to come home. He made us go to bed, we were so worried about you Beth." Her eyes filled; she must be strong for her family thought Beth. Meg glanced out the window. "You have to go Beth, he may come back and do it," she cried. So Beth got her mother settled in bed and went with her sister Meg. With a heavy and broken heart, she talked to her sister. And then it was decided that she must sneak out the back window, as she did not want to go out the front door, as he could be waiting there.

They said tearful good-byes, and Beth hit the ground running. She was terrified now as he may see her and shoot her. She did not trust her father now, or ever again. She vowed as she ran like a scared deer in the night that she would never see him again. The thick mist and fog was rolling in off the lake as she ran into the night. She eventually slowed into a walk to the next town, which was where her other sister lived. She ran until she felt safe. She lost track of all time as she felt like she was the only person in the world. The darkness lay all around her, but she was not afraid. The mist shrouded her as she looked to the heavens and whispered "please god help me, and protect my family."

Suddenly she saw car lights coming toward her. She felt panic as she was all alone on a highway. She hid behind a tree as they passed by. She figured that it was a bunch of miners going home from work. But a strange thing happened; they came back for her. In their lights, they could see a frightened young girl. They stopped and stared in astonishment at this young girl walking alone on the highway in the predawn hours. She stared at these people and knew they were from her hometown. One of them in particular was a person who knew Harry well. "You are Harry's sister, aren't you?" he asked. Beth nodded. "Get in," he said. "We will take you home."

"No," Beth replied. "I need to get to my sister's in the next town."

"Okay," he replied, noticing that she was almost in shock, "we will do this for you." Sometime later they dropped her off to her sister's place. She thought she thanked them but was not sure. The one who knew her brother walked her to the door. "Take care of yourself," he said. "I don't know what the problem is, but good luck." Beth was sobbing as a shocked Amy answered the door in the dawning hour.

"Where did you come from?" she asked, hugging her sister close. She was shocked at the way her sister looked; she was white as a sheet and shaking. She could not believe it when Beth told her everything, and that she walked all night to get there. She got her settled into bed. Amy knew what her father was like as she too had left at an early age to get away from the misery that was their lives.

The next morning, Beth called her mom to say that she was all right. Her mother was heartbroken that her daughter had to run away from her own home. Beth promised that one day that she would come home, but she never did, not for many years. She did not want to see him ever again, for to her he was dead. She stayed with her sister, helping around the house and doing odd jobs. She did not know what she wanted to do with her life as it had been in turmoil all these years. She didn't know who she was anymore. Her sister Amy suggested that she get a job in a store or something, to help out the town was bigger than hers, but still there was not much to do there. Her sister was having babies close together; she was getting a large family also. Her husband was running around on Amy. She may have known this, for there were many arguments. However, Beth knew for she had seen him with another woman, but did not want to hurt her sister, by telling her.

The anger and disgust got the better of her one day, and she told him off and left the household. She then stayed with her other sister Jenna for the next few years. She got into photography and learned everything she could and was very good at it. As time went on, Jenna started to try and match Beth with this nice guy that they knew for a long time. Beth was not too interested as she wanted to get her career going in photography, but she did agree to meet this person and get it over with. They had planned to go to dinner that evening, and Beth had a new dress that she was waiting for an occasion to wear. So that weekend the guy came to the door. Henry was a quiet, soft-spoken guy. Beth's first impression of him was that he was one of those really quite, easy going guys. He said all the right things and all, but as time went on, he was very persistent in his personality, so Beth liked his sincerity and mannerisms. She found herself falling in love with him.

Of course, her sister was delighted over this and encouraged it to the max. After a two-year courtship, Henry and Beth married and settled down to a happy life. Beth was the happiest that she had ever been. In the following years, they had five children and were finally a real family. As the children got older, Beth decided to start her own business in photography. But to her surprise, Henry said that she did not need a business as he made enough to support his family. Beth was surprised at this reaction as they taught the children that they could achieve anything they put their minds to, so she let it go. As the children grew up and started leaving home to go on with their lives, Beth could feel a slight strain between her and Henry. They did not seem to be as close now as Henry was in construction. He was working away on different new projects. Beth was a little resentful as he was away seeing new things and meeting new people, and here she was home with their youngest child, who was getting ready to move out. The stress level was high. Sometimes she wanted him to be working closer to the family, but as first foreman with the company, he was sent out of town to supervise new jobs. But she felt a little guilty at times also—after all, he was doing it for them.

The last of their children moved away to start her own life. It was the following year that Beth, after many discussions with her husband, decided to get her business going. It took many months to get it off the ground, and she was very excited. One day Henry said, "Maybe we should go for a vacation before we get too busy this summer." Beth was all excited about this as they had never had a honeymoon after they married.

Her friend Rita had stopped by the business and asked her to go to lunch. She was very nice, but hated all men in general, as her husband had taken off with her own sister, with whom Rita had not spoken to in many years. She was a bitter lady. Beth felt guilty sometimes as she and Henry were so happy.

Her days were filled with getting ready for their trip to the mountains. Beth had never traveled anywhere before as the children had come so quickly. She looked forward to being all alone with her husband in a lovely setting. One day before the trip, they went out to dinner to celebrate her success at the business; she had done very well in one year. Henry brought roses and candy to the restaurant; he was in a very happy mood, as was Beth. They talked and laughed all the way through. She went to the powder room, smiling at how wonderful life was if you are with the right person. She thought about poor Rita and decided to spend more time with her,

When they got back from vacation, she was thinking about it all, as she would ask Henry to help find Rita some nice person, for Henry had a lot of good, decent men friends. As she came out of the powder room, she stopped. There was a pretty redheaded woman sitting at their table. Her instinct was to pull back and watch. The woman was smiling into her husband's eyes, as she laid her hand on his, still smiling. Beth stood there, not knowing what to do. Suddenly the woman got up and left rather quickly. Henry watched her like a schoolboy as she disappeared around the corner.

Beth acted casual as she walked to the table. "Who is the pretty redhead?" she asked with a stiff smile.

He smiled broadly. "Oh, that's Bonnie from the insurance office. She works for the company part-time. She is the company's insurance agent." Beth smiled. Henry went on, "We met at the bosses' office one day. She stopped by, she thought I was eating lunch alone and wanted to keep me company."

"I see." Beth smiled again.

"Well, honey, I have to get back to work," he said, and as Beth had to finish her inventory, she had to go too. They said good-byes, and each went their separate ways. *At least*, Beth thought, *this shortens my day*. The time went by fast as Beth was now busy getting her staff in place before their vacation, and Henry was working evenings, to catch up on his workload before the trip. So Beth had lots of time on her hands to do her shopping and get some time in with Rita. She mentioned to her about the redhead who came to the restaurant.

"You watch that one," she warned Beth. "She is a man-eater. She has been involved with many men in the past. Some say she even killed a person, and that she was in a mental facility for some years."

Beth could not believe what Rita was telling her. "Look," Rita said, after noticing the look on Beths face, "all I am saying is, watch your man, for I would not let her near my husband if I were you."

It gave Beth something to think about as she drove home that evening. She decided to pick up some pizza for her and Henry, as she did not feel like cooking today. She smiled to herself. *I'm on vacation time already*, as it was two days before they were to leave. She pulled into the parking lot of the pizza place and made her way inside. The place was very busy, so she sat and waited to order. She looked around casually. People did not want to cook, she thought, as it was hot outside and in here was so cool. She got up to go to the powder room, and when she did, she happened to glance to the left side of the room and stood rooted there in shock. There was her husband and that redhead sitting together, and they were so involved with each other that they did not notice Beth standing there or anyone else for that matter. The woman was pawing her husband, and he was enjoying it.

She made a very fast exit to the back door, which was behind her, and stumbled outside. She could not believe what her eyes had seen. Her Henry and another woman. She turned and watched as Henry kissed her in a passion that he had not displayed to Beth in a very long time. A Jealous rage welled up in her heart now as she watched her husband get personal with this woman, as his hand moved on her long, slim leg as she crossed them. She could not stand there any longer; she sat in her vehicle and waited as they left. She was going to follow, but her pride forbade it.

That night Henry came home and Beth was sleeping. He took a quick shower and slept on the couch. He thought that if Beth found out about the cheating, they would be finished—and he did not want this to happen; he was not ready as yet. First, he had to talk to an accountant for Beth's business, one who would go along with both their ideas, as Beth was trying to do it all by herself, but that was not the real reason.

Beth awoke; it was late, and Henry was not home yet. Anger and pain was going through her as she went downstairs to have a coffee, thinking that he was probably still out with her. She went into the living room to watch the news, and there she found Henry, sleeping on the couch.

He heard a noise and opened his eyes. "Oh, hon," he said, "I came home late and didn't want to disturb you, so I decided to bunk on the couch."

"How considerate of you, Henry," she retorted angrily. He looked at her. "What is wrong?"

Beth was getting angry now. "Tell me, how long have you been cheating on me?" she asked. Henry turned red, then pale. He avoided her stare, "How long have you known?" he asked.

"Answer my question, Henry." Beth slammed her fist on the table. "Do you have any idea of how I felt when I saw my husband cuddling up in a public place with that redhead?" He could not answer. "I have a choice for you, Henry. We are going to get marriage counseling or we divorce—that is your choice." She went upstairs, slamming the door and locking it. *He can sleep on the couch all the time for what I care*, she thought angrily.

It was the following week that Henry wanted to talk to his wife. "Beth, I'm sorry, honey, but I am only human, and it will never happen again, I swear. It was just a fling. We will go to marriage counseling if you want, honey, I don't want to lose you. I love you. We have been married twenty-five years, why throw all those beautiful memories away?"

Beth was in tears now as she was very hurt and angry over his infidelity. The next day, Henry canceled the trip at Beth's request as they made arrangements to go into counseling. After many months, things were almost back to normal. Henry was the ideal husband, home after work every day and he did not do any more night shifts. Beth was very happy but it would be sometime before she really trusted him again.

One day Henry said, "I want to invite a friend of mine and his wife to come to dinner. He is an accountant, and I thought that maybe you would be interested in hiring him to do the books. This way we can be free to spend more time together."

Beth smiled and agreed. "I would like that," she said.

That following Friday the couple came to dinner. Don was a nice man and seemed to know his job, but beth could tell he was a drinker from the beginning. His wife Annie was a quiet woman and very friendly. She reminded Beth of her mother, she took an instant liking to her. As time went on, the four friends spent a lot of time together and became like a family. Each did different events, and the others were always there. "That's the way friends should be," Henry commented one time. "Yes," agreed Beth. The business was very successful now as Beth put her all into it, and it was paying off. Don knew all about how succesful it was and said, "It's a strong, going concern and you have made it what it is, Beth, be proud of that."

Don liked to drink more than the ordinary person, but he knew his work, and Beth was happy with him. One day she came home early to find Don and Henry sitting on the deck, laughing very hard at something. Beth came around the corner with a smile. "What's up?" she asked, still smiling. Don smirked. "Oh, your husband is planning a takeover of a business."

Henry gave him a dirty look, glancing quickly toward Beth. "Don't mind him, Beth. He has had too much to drink."

"Where is Annie?" asked Beth, puzzled by their behavior.

"She went home to get some things to help make supper," Don replied. The evening ended with Annie driving her husband home. Before Don left, he said, "Don't forget to tell Beth about the skiing trip."

Beth smiled and replied, "He will have a bad head in the morning."

Henry looked at her and changed the subject. "We are planning a ski trip. I want you to learn how to ski." He laughed.

Beth was confused. "May I ask why?" She smiled.

"Oh, our trip is going be the four of us, and they know how to ski, so I don't want you to be left out. So I have hired one of the best instructors up there. She will teach you all you need to know," he replied.

Beth kissed him. "You are the most considerate husband, honey. I love you." "Well," he replied "this is our honeymoon, but with friends around to celebrate."

That's why their marriage was more solid than ever, Beth thought. But she was not prepared for what was in store. The ski travelling trip took hours, it seemed to Beth. She was tired of the long drive, but once they arrived, she loved it all. It was a chateau setting with amber lights sparkling on the snow. She felt like she was in a dream and their suite was out of this world, with a heart-shaped tub and lots of marble. The king-sized bed looked so inviting to Beth that she wanted to lie down. But Henry said that they had made plans for a sleigh ride. Beth was so happy to have such a thoughtful husband, her world was wonderful, or so she thought, for "under every silver lining lies a snake within."

They had dinner, then went on a romantic sleigh ride. Beth smiled happily as Henry hummed a song to her. The following morning, they all set out for the slopes. Beth was worried about learning to ski; she did not relish the thought of going down a big hill. But her fears were put to rest as the female instructor had her start on the kiddies' slope the first time. She felt a little silly doing that while the others skied normally on the big one, but within a week Beth had learned enough to ski with the others. She was so proud of this and was anxious to show them what she could do. The instructor went along with her to guide her down the slope, but Beth wanted to go alone on the next one. The instructor pointed to where she was to ski down, and Beth excitedly went, again on her own. The others were way ahead of her, but she smiled. *Maybe I can catch up to them*, she thought.

She left the hill and skied down to where the instructor had told her to go. She passed a couple and then was skiing by herself as there seemed to be a different route she was going. The snow was so bright now. Suddenly she came upon a sign that said Danger: Do Not Enter; Beth panicked; she was moving very fast toward the danger area and could not seem to stop. Suddenly one of her skis hit a bump that was under the snow. She went down tumbling on her front and flipping over and down in a vicious slide. The memory of that will always stay with her as she finally came to a stop not two feet from a ninety-foot drop to the side. It must have been hours before the ski patrol found her. She was scraped badly in her face, and her leg was badly hurt. They said she was very lucky as the drop would have been a sure death. She was brought to the hospital by helicopter, and was examined. There were more bruises, but other than that she was all right.

Henry and their friends did not know that she had gone down again, as they were planning on taking another run and then finish the day. They thought that she had gone inside. They were horrified when they learned of the direction she had gone, but it was a happy evening when they brought her back safe and sound. They had given her something to help her calm down and sleep. Henry got her settled in bed, and Annie sat with her for a while as Henry went to get her prescription filled.

He went to a fifth door in the hotel, and knocked. Bonnie answered, wearing a skimpy outfit. Henry quickly stepped inside and grabbed her in his arms. After a long passionate kiss, he said, "We failed today."

"Yes," replied Bonnie. She smiled nastily. "But the next plan will do it, for I have hired a friend of mine for you, she is becoming a thorn in my side," she said with a sneer.

"I spoke to him already," Henry replied. "We have a lot of money tied up in this."

Bonnie smirked. "Yes, four million dollars worth."

Henry left there around dawn as by now Beth would be looking for him. He would pretend that he went for a run as he could not sleep. Beth had awakened some time ago. She called for her husband, but there was no response. She figured that he had fallen asleep on the lounger as he maybe did not want to awaken her. She grimaced in pain as her foot was throbbing terribly and her face was stiff and painful. She fell back to sleep again as she had taken a sedative that lay on the night table, as Annie had gotten some for her while Henry was out. The following morning found Beth in extreme pain. Henry pretended that the drugstore had been closed last night; therefore, he could not get it filled, and that yes, he had come back and checked on her and had slept on the lounger as Beth had thought. Annie came by to see her and decided to go and get the prescription filled for her friend. She would stay with her now as Henry had some things to do with Don, Annie's husband.

Don and Henry went to get some breakfast together, and the conversation came up with Don inquiring, "Have you decided to do the takeover yet?"

"Well, we now have to wait until her foot heals," he replied. "No need tell her while she is in pain."

Don smiled. "What a surprise it's going to be when she finds out that she did not sign all of the documents making the company hers." He laughed nastily.

Henry liked Don as he knew he was unscrupulous when he got Beth to hire him. He smiled in return. "Yes, I will have it all." They both laughed and toasted each other with a coffee. In the following months, Beth and

Henry were constantly arguing about things that to Beth did not seem that important. Things like what time she got home in the evenings and her spending too much time with Annie and Rita. Henry seemed to want to argue all of the time these days. Beth could not understand how someone could change in a few months' time.

The day finally came when Beth got the shock of her life. She had gone into town to get some purchases for the office, and when she arrived home, there was Don and her husband sitting on the deck. Henry greeted her with an explanation of how he told the boss that he was sick. Beth looked at Don.

"And what was your excuse?" She smiled.

"Oh, I'm on my own." He snickered. "I can come and go as I please."

Beth had to admit it was a beautiful day, too nice to be working. "So I guess we are going to barbecue?" She glanced at her husband.

"Yes," he smiled, "that is right." Beth went to change and to get things started. She called Annie to come over, as her husband was there, she informed her. Annie was quiet on the other end.

Beth asked, "Did you hear me, Annie?" After a brief silence, Annie responded, "Yes, Beth, I will be there."

Beth asked, "Are you all right, Annie?"

"Yes," replied Annie, "it's just that Don has been taking a lot of days off and not telling me about it, or where he goes when he does."

Beth said, "Come over and we will talk."

The evening was a little tense as Annie was annoyed with her husband. Don seemed to drink more as it wore on, and Henry was keeping up. The women went inside to chat because the stereo was too loud to hear each other on the deck. Annie confided to Beth that Don was having dreams now in his drunken state ,something about a takeover, she was not sure who it was but she said that she was considering, divorceing her husband because of his drinking as they were drifting apart. After some time, they came outside, and the men were really partying. Beth turned down the music. Don had a sly look on his face as he glanced at Henry. "Aren't you going to tell her now about the takeover?" he asked Henry.

Her husband glanced nervously at Beth, but before he could respond, Don blurted out in a drunken manner, "Your husband has taken over your business as of nine this morning." He snickered, truly enjoying the look of shock on Beth's face. She stood there as if in a daze.

"Is this true?" she asked her husband. "Have you taken my business from me?" Her voice was rising now. "How can you do that? I signed all documents to the effect, and making you a partner in it," she said.

Don suddenly guffawed, "No, you didn't." He laughed. "You did not sign the most important one. Now he can legally take it, and he has." He went off into another bout of laughter as poor Beth stood there staring at the man she married so many years ago.

"How could you do this to me?" she asked shakily. "What kind of man are you?" With that, she got into her car with Annie close behind her, and went to try and find the documents that were not signed. She was so upset that Annie insisted on driving the rest of the way. When they arrived in town, the lawyer's office was closed. Beth was so upset that Annie had her come to a coffee café to talk it out; her heart was breaking for her friend's misery.

Beth asked, "How can someone you love do such a horrible thing?" Annie could not answer. She knew that Beth had a very hard life growing up and that she had put her whole being into this little business of hers, and now for the one person in the world to betray her like this was horrible—her own husband.

"You know, sometimes we think we really know someone, but then we discover that they are wolves in sheep's clothing," Annie replied, and Beth nodded miserably.

The next morning, Beth called her lawyer and set up an immediate appointment. "Mrs. Lobee, the document that you did not sign came to me from your bank sometime ago. I thought you knew about it and would be in to sign it—yes, your husband can and, according to the notice I received this morning, has taken your business as you were supposed to sign the documents making you the owner and your husband partner. When the signing is not finalized, this is what can occur." He glanced at her in pity.

Beth left the office with tears in her eyes. She felt so betrayed by someone whom she thought would never hurt her. When she arrived home, Henry was nowhere to be seen. When he did come home at last, he came into the kitchen and said, "You have to sign this document saying that you are now an employee of the company."

Beth stared at him in anger. "You want me to be an employee of my own company? How dare you to do this to me! I built this business out of scratch and did not expect my own husband to take it away from me." She angrily tore the document to shreds. "You tell that crooked accountant friend of yours that I'm not signing anything, and that is final."

She walked out onto the deck. It was a warm, sunny morning. Beth loved to sit there that time of the day as it was peaceful as she listened to the gurgling of the little brook. But this morning brought no solace as the turmoil inside her was evident. Henry ignored her all that day and into the next.

He had gone to work one morning, and Beth decided to go to her business. But when she got there, the locks had been changed. Beth was so angry and hurt over this that she called a locksmith and had it changed back to her code. Henry called her around lunchtime to inform her that he had changed the code, and that the locksmith had been told not to touch it again at anyone's request.

She felt her world tumbling down around her now as the one thing that had kept her happy besides her husband was her little business. She was so proud of that as she had a very hard life, and Henry knew that this was part of her survival. But he tried to reason with her, "it's still yours, or ours now." One day Beth came home to what she thought was an empty house. She assumed that her husband was at work as the car was not there. Beth walked toward the stairs. Suddenly she heard a sound; it was coming from the living room. She walked quietly and rounded the corner. There was her husband, talking on the phone. He had his back to her, so she crept quietly upstairs and picked up the extension. *If it's that girl, I will give her a piece of my mind*, she thought angrily. But what she heard made her anxious and puzzled. Her husband was saying, "Meet me on the dock at midnight, and I will give you all the information."

The voice on the other end replied in a raspy voice, "What do you want me to do with the body?" Her blood ran cold, as she realized that her husband was up to something terrible.

"We will discuss that when you get here, and don't be late," her husband said. This sounded like a hired killer.//

Beth was as pale as a ghost as she laid the receiver back down. Her husband was going to get her killed by a hit man. She could not think as she sagged against the bed, sick now to her stomach. Suddenly she heard her name. "Beth, are you home? Come have your coffee."

This was their favourite time of the evening she looked forward to having the coffee on the deck facing the little brook. She sank onto the bed now with rubbery legs that would not move. Suddenly he was there staring at her.

"Beth, I called you. Are you not feeling well? You look like you have seen a ghost." Beth forced herself to look him in the face, as with a faint feeling she tried to stand up to go downstairs. He was so concerned for her well-being that it was hard to believe what she had just heard, but she must act as normal as possible. He must not know that she overheard. She went downstairs over his objections of trying to get her to lie down. They sat and had their coffee, and Beth tried to act as normal as possible, saying that she must be getting the stomach flu as that was the truth in a way. She felt like vomiting, sitting here with a potential killer.

She excused herself, saying that she would lie down after all. She went upstairs on wobbly legs and collapsed on the bed in tears. She stared at their wedding photo that she had so lovingly ordered especially for the photo, and her children's photos. She thought, *I have to let my children know what's happening. I have to get help.* Quietly she crept downstairs to find Henry sleeping in a chair on the deck. She walked quickly out the door and toward the highway as she did not want to start the car, for he would hear. She walked in tears toward the main road, all the while remembering that this seemed to be her way of life, having to run away to survive.

Here I go again, she thought. Some twenty-five years later, her heart was broken again. Suddenly a truck came careening around the corner. She jumped to the side of the road. The truck had an out-of-town license plate, and she got a glimpse of the driver. He had a dirty headband on and had a gray-looking beard. He looked at her quickly and was on his way. *Some drivers*, she thought, *they needed to be locked up*. It was some hours later, it seemed, that Beth checked into a hotel room. She would stay there for the night. But the thought kept nagging at her to go back, that if she ran away, Henry would know that she had heard the conversation, so she checked out and got a cab home. Luckily, Henry was drinking now and had no idea that she had left, and their friend Don had come out to visit. They only lived about three miles from town; lots of times in summer Beth biked to town for the exercise.

Beth said hello to their accountant and left them to talk. *Probably about me.* She shuddered about tonight as she was not sure if Henry was talking about her to the hit man or someone else. He seemed genuinely concerned about her welfare. *Maybe I'm wrong*, she thought. *Oh God, I hope so.* She stayed in the room until she heard Don leave, then she went downstairs to find Henry staring off into the night.

"I have to go take care of some business," he said suddenly. "Don't wait up." And he was gone. Beth thought, *What is going on with this man?* She did not know him anymore. She would go tomorrow and file for divorce. She waited for him that night, but he did not show up until dawn. Beth watched him walk into the room. She sat there and waited for him to say something, but he just glanced her way, as if he expected her to be sitting there at this late hour.

"Henry," she raised her voice, "I am filing for divorce." At this news he stopped in his tracks and spun around.

"You what?" he asked.

Beth stared him in the face. "We have nothing between us anymore, and I need to have my life back and go on to start a new one." Her voice was now hoarse with emotion. "You left me a long time ago, Henry. I cannot continue like this." Her eyes filled with tears. "I'm done," she said with a ring of finality in her voice.

Henry stared down at the floor. As he listened to all of her words, his mind was spinning now as he had to keep her around to get the job done.

"Beth"—he stopped and looked confused—"I may not be the best husband lately, but I do love you. I need you to be there for me. Hell, I'm sorry I took your business, but I felt less of a man whenever the guys called me 'Mrs. Lobee,' and as I said before its ours now, and I have changed the code back to yours at the business."

Beth did not say a word as she got up and left the room, leaving Henry to wonder if he made any impact. It was a few months later that Henry announced that one of his friends had a cabin in the country, and as it was coming to hunting season, he wanted Beth to come along with them. He said it would do her some good to get away from it all. Beth had put the divorce on hold for the time being, but she did not tell Henry this. The following week, Beth was packing to go to this cabin. There were others coming along as well. She wanted to know if there would be other females going, and Henry assured her that yes, there were wives coming too.

She was happily looking around as they drove through the lovely countryside. It was the end of September now, and the leaves were turning into the fall colors. Beth liked this time of year; the colors were wonderful to see. They finally arrived to a lovely big cabin that spread a half mile wide on either side and was laid out like a modern-style ranch. It was so big that Beth could not see any surroundings right away, but then they pulled into a large driveway. It was breathtaking.

The cabin was landscaped to perfection on either side. The front had lions on either side of the wrought-iron gates. One lady said as she came to where Beth was standing, gazing at it all, "This guy must be loaded. This is good enough to be in the city."

"Yes," Beth agreed with delight, "it sure is a surprise to be finding something like this in the middle of the woods." She introduced herself, and so did the other two ladies. Maud and Sheila and Betty seemed to be very nice. Beth happily thought, *I can go hiking every day here,* as that had become part of her life now. She noticed a couple of guesthouses also at the rear of the cabin. The scenery was out of this world, she thought as she looked to the rear. It had land for miles and large trees surrounding the outback area.

They had not seen the inside as yet. Beth gasped at what she saw as they entered the large foyer. There were spiraling staircases on either side of the foyer leading up to the top level, and marble everywhere. Her eyes looked at flowers and statues and pictures all laid out like it was a grand manor. Beth thought, *It is a grand manor, only in the country.* The ladies went to pick their bedrooms, which had all the expensive comforts of home, and then some. They all settled in to each other's rooms, and the ladies were delighted with the very large kitchen that had every food stuff that a person could want. This was like a wonderful dream, thought Beth.

She had thought that they were coming to a plain old hunting cabin. She mentioned as much to Henry, but he laughed and replied, "I had seen pictures of this but wanted to surprise you. Sam, the owner, will be coming up later in the week."

Night fell, and the friends had the outdoor lighting on, and the barbecues were on. The starry night and full moon made this the perfect place to be honeymooning, thought Beth as she sat and took it all in. The next morning found Beth bathing in a very lovely, deep tub. She did not want to get out as it was so fancy to her. She finished and then decided to explore. The other ladies wanted to stay around the deck, which was all right with Beth. She set out to the rear to get a good look at the guesthouse. She was ambling along, not moving too fast as the scenery was breathtaking. She walked toward one of the guest homes and thought she saw a face looking out at her. The sun was very bright. As she looked closer, sure enough there was a movement in there. She mentioned this to Henry later in the evening, but he said that she must have been mistaken, for these houses were not to be occupied until next month because Sam, the owner, rented them out to other hunters every season.

Beth was puzzled but curious. Well, she would go there again and peek in the windows. Henry had told her to stay around with the others as it was hunting season, and that it was dangerous around that area. She decided to go for a hike instead. The other ladies, sort of kept busy at home getting dinners cooked, and it seemed to Beth that none of them were the exploring type. But they were very friendly and assured Beth that later they would all go with her for a long walk. She started out along a little trail that was running behind the guest homes. There was a peaceful silence now as she walked in a relaxed manner. She loved the outdoors and relished every moment of it. This trail was taking her out to a wider area as it had turns and a winding road that took her away from the property now. Suddenly she stopped.

She heard running water. She decided to follow the sound and came upon the loveliest little stream that ran along a bank. It was man-made, she could tell, but her most pleasant surprise was the animals in the pasture. She smiled as she looked over there. There were horses and cows and even a couple of llamas. She sat by the stream and listened as it gurgled. *This will be my little getaway.* She smiled, gazing contentedly at the scene that lay before her. Suddenly a shot rang out. It seemed that it was close in her direction. Beth fell to the ground in fright. There was no sign of anyone around, but she surmised that it came from the heavily treed area. She felt a little pain something gushing in her leg and looked in horror. She realized that she was bleeding.

"Oh God," she screamed, "I have been hit!" Henry had warned her. She struggled to get up, but it was too hard. She laid there now in panic and pain. What if no one found her? She would bleed to death. She grabbed her backpack, which was nearby and got out her bandage. She always brought her pack of emergency things with her as she often thought anything can happen on a hike. And now it did, she bandaged her leg as tight as she could to stop the bleeding. She tried to stand but could not; the pain was too great. She thought, *There is a bullet in my body.* It seemed like hours to Beth now as she sat there in a panic, as the animals were coming to drink. She did not know how these animals would react to the smell of blood as it was all over the grassy knoll that she lay on.

Henry had come home early from hunting as he wanted to spend time with his wife. The ladies were sitting outside, enjoying the sun, but Beth was not there. Henry could not see Beth sitting around like that as she liked to be busy.

"Where is Beth?" He smiled. "Upstairs?" he asked. Maude, the older lady, replied, "No, she went hiking hours ago."

In a little panic he replied, "Hiking! I have to go find her as there are hunters around and it's dangerous out there." He quickly got to the direction of where she had gone and set out.

Beth tried to move as quickly as possible, all the while crying in panic as the animals were now sort of running and wagging tails to the water spot. Her panic was getting the best of her. "I must keep a cool head." she thought.

Henry called her name loudly, but there was no response. He thought she must be farther away than he assumed. Suddenly he stopped in his tracks, for he heard a woman scream. He listened to find what direction the sound had come from. He ran towards the sound.

"Beth!"

He finally came to a clearing by which he found his wife, passed out and bloody.

"Beth!"

He ran to her side, noticing that she was bleeding profusely, even though she had bandaged it. He looked around quickly. The animals were trying to drink, and they seemed confused. "Go," he shooed them away.

"Beth," he called her name, "wake up." But she had fainted he had to find some way to get her home from here. He called another hunter from the cabin on his radio, and within a half hour, they had Beth on a quad and on her way back home. The ladies were very upset at the news that she had been shot. Maude was a retired nurse; she cleaned Beth's injury, then Henry drove back to the city to get her care at emergency. Of course, it had to be reported to the police for the records. Any shooting or accident on these hunts had to be written up.

At midnight Henry was on the way home with his wife. They had taken the bullet out and had cleaned and bandaged the wound. Beth would not be going anywhere for a while. After getting Beth settled in bed with the help of the other ladies who were anxious to help, Henry said, "I am going for a walk."

He walked around the cabin and knocked on the door of the second guesthouse. There was a very dim light showing through the window. The door opened, and a man in dirty jeans and headband stood aside to let him in. Henry turned toward him. "Why didn't you finish the job?" He angrily asked.

The man looked around, confused. "I did kill her," he replied.

"No, you did not," Henry retorted. "She is lying at the cabin with a bullet wound in her leg and still alive. I have contracted you to do this—at a big expense, I might add—and I expect for you to finish this."

The man stared and replied, "She went down when I fired. I waited, and she didn't get up, so I figured that it was finished."

"Pardon the pun, my friend, but not by a long shot is it finished."

Henry walked toward the door to leave. With his back to the other man, he said, "When she gets on her feet, I expect you to fully carry out my request. Is that clear, Mr. Clum?" The man nodded, and replied yes sir.

Wayne ronald Clum had been in and out of prison since he was a child of fourteen. His father abused his son by making him live on the streets to bring home money and drugs, and his mother ran off with another man, which made his father even meaner to this lonely boy. After getting out of a youth facility, for trying to kill his father, sometime later he met up with some people who were in the underground connection of killers for hire. There were some, as young as twelve in this connection, he was.

His first job was to kill his cousin, whom he hated, and then he was on his way to a life of crime. He found out after the killings that he liked what he did, it gave him a satisfaction, just watching them die. As he got older, he moved all over the world on killing sprees as he called it. Now he was here to take care of this woman. He had a picture but had never seen her face close-up. But he snickered. That will come as he loved to watch them as they died. This man was proud of what he did for a living, and he was one the best. In the following days, Beth was healing fast. She did not want people fussing over her. As much as they meant well, she was very independent and wanted to do things on her own.

Maude and the other two ladies were constantly checking on her and doing everything they could for her, to which she appreciated. As she healed, she could not help but notice that her husband was gone a lot. She questioned him one day, and in a cold tone, his response was, "I have to go hunting with the guys—after all, that's why we are here."

Beth felt a little guilty sitting there and not being able to do things for him. But Maude, Sheila, and Betty assured her that he was being taken care of. Beth was glad to have these women with her. Otherwise, she would have been very lonely by herself, with the men gone all day until nightfall. Into her sixth week, Beth was able to walk again; her leg was a little stiff, as it had not been used for a long time. The girls helped her down to the exercise room every day to work on the leg. As Maude was a nurse, she knew what to do to help her get her body back in shape. It was awhile before Beth could go outside again. She finally got to go on the day before they were to leave for town. She felt upset that she did not get to go hiking again, but Henry assured her that they would indeed come again. Beth was happy about this as she loved the outdoors, especially in this setting.

Wayne Ronald clum was advised by Henry the night before that they would be leaving in the morning. He packed up his belongings and weapon and moved out that night before anyone could see him. He was to do the job back in the town. If Beth could have seen that old truck that was tucked away behind the guesthouse number 2, she would have been suspicious and told Henry, and all would have been hard to figure out to satisfy her curiosity.

It had been many months since Beth had overheard the conversation between her husband and this killer. She had to talk to him as she was very afraid to live a normal life, and the divorce was on hold for now, but it depended on his response to what she was going to ask. That evening she sat across from her husband. She took a deep breath and said, "Henry, I have to tell you something to which I'm very scared to receive an answer to." Beth got Henry's attention just by the way she said this.

"Go ahead, Beth, you don't have to be scared of anything," he replied.

"Well"—and she got up and walked toward the window, trying to control her tears—"I came home one day and thought you were at work, but I overheard you talking on the phone—," she stopped and glanced nervously in his direction.

"Go on," Henry said in a quiet voice.

She said, "I heard you talking to a man who sounded like a killer or something . . . and you wanted him to do something for you."

"And that was . . . ?" Henry asked in a tone that was a little edgy. She glanced at his face; there was no emotion there.

"I heard him asking you what to do with the body," she answered quickly. Her heart was beating so fast that she was sure that he heard it. The was a brief silence as Beth waited for his reply. Suddenly the silence was broken with laughter. She stared at her husband as he guffawed so loud that she started to laugh also. In confusion, Beth stopped. Henry looked at her, still smiling.

"Oh, Beth," he replied laughingly, "That was a recorded set line that I did for our friend Sam. Did I not mention that he is a mystery writer? That was a demo I did for him, and that was him on the other end that you heard. We did it to get the recording for his movie script that he is doing, for his book."

Beth laughed. "And all this time I was going to divorce you and leave this town, thinking that you hired a killer to get rid of me." She was crying and laughing at the same time.

"Oh, honey, I would not hurt a hair on your lovely head," he said as he took her into his arms, closing his eyes in relief at the quick answer that he came up with.

Later in the evening Henry went into town. Beth smiled. "Bring back some shampoo, honey," she said. He was going bowling with the boys, his hunting buddies, for a few hours. Beth called the girls and arranged to have lunch with them the following day. She just wanted to stay at home, reveling in her husband's love for her.

Henry drove into town thinking that was too close, and that he must be careful from now on. He parked beside a wrought-iron gate and walked to the house. She opened the door and received him as always, dressed nicely in heels as she knew he wanted that.

"Well, I have a surprise for you, Bonnie," he said after much time in the bedroom.

"Oh, what is that, my love?" she asked. "Are you going to tell me that your wifey is dead?" she snickered.

"No," Henry said, "but she overheard me talking to Wayne and confronted me out of the blue today. We must be very careful from now on. No talking on the phone about anything other than ordinary things, as she may be listening in, as bonnie had called several times to their home about the business .and henry had always answered. On second thought, don't call the house." he suggested.

Bonnie snorted in a very unladylike way. "Now she has taken to listening in on conversations. What a bitch," she said as she plopped herself down on his lap.

Beth thought, *I will surprise my hubby and make him a special meal.* She smiled at his surprise when he arrived home. She got busy now, making the meal and lighting candles all around the living room and kitchen area. When he arrived, she had planned on turning off all the lights and having a candlelit dinner. *Very romantic*, she thought, *we have not been together in a long time.* After some time, as Beth was getting the finishing touches done to the dinner, she heard a noise. *That's him!* she thought excitedly. She rushed to turn off the lights and waited for his footsteps, but there was none.

She peeked outside, and to her horror, there was that old truck that she had seen on their property before. Grabbing the phone, she called Henry on his cell; there was no answer. In a panic she ran around, turning on all the lights and even the spotlight outside to let this guy know that she knew that he was there. In fear and exhaustion, she sank into a chair, looking out from between the blinds. He was still standing there under the big tree. His truck was running, as if he was ready to take off in a hurry. She called Henry again—no answer. Suddenly there was a loud noise, and as she looked out, he was taking off at a very fast speed. She must tell Henry about this as it had happened before. Something strange was going on.

Many hours later Henry arrived. He had met with Wayne ronald clum that night and arranged to stop the contract on his wife, as she was not well. He even paid him extra, but this killer had a signed contract, and secretly he would carry it out. The meal that she had prepared so lovingly was thrown in the garbage as Beth was now in tears. She felt abandoned as her husband had come home and did not even listen to what she had to say, nor did he even give her a glance. He went upstairs, and she could hear the shower running. She felt as small as a crumb as she lay on the couch where she stayed that night.

The embarrassment of getting declothed in front of her husband was now a shame to her as she felt that he did not want her anymore, and she wondered in tears what she had done. Maybe there was still another woman. But Beth was the kind of woman who had pride and respect for herself as a woman, and she did not take things lying down, as she stood on her own two feet—and that thought had crossed her mind many times about his infidelity. But she would give him the benefit of the doubt.

The years went by and Henry and Beth were still together, for Beth had not wanted to leave her home as she had nowhere that she wanted to go. She lived on the good memories that they had in the beginning. As they were both much older now, it seemed right to stay together. Bonnie had become an important part of Henry's life for she was the one he spent all his time with, as he and Beth were strangers, living in the same house, Beth knew now that there was another woman as he did not hide much. She thought sometimes that he left signs so she would find it, but as time went on, Beth decided that she would divorce him after all. It took many months and days to get it all over and done with. Beth got to keep her house by the brook as that was all she wanted. She would survive on her alimony, and she also had savings. Beth had the children come for visits now as she found it lonely, and she wrote this in her diary and had arranged for her daughter Michelle to get it in her will. Michelle was concerned about her mother living alone, so she moved out to that province to be near her. She now lived in a little town where she could visit on a regular time, which was every second of the month, as she was very busy with her own career.

One day she called her mother, and her mom tried to sound happy, but Michelle knew that she was not. Her father had his own life with this other woman and did not even try to contact his children, it seemed like he was no longer their father.

Winter was coming on, and Beth was getting things ready for winter. The colors of fall were splendid as she sat on her deck and looked around. She was getting up in age; she could feel it now as the days passed. She tried to keep busy, but it was getting harder. But Beth was tough; she was not giving up, for Beth did not fall to her knees for the world. She discovered a long time ago that when anything good happened to a person, or that if you were happy, it seemed that no one wanted much to do with you. Or so that's the human way, it seemed to her, in her world of friends and even distant family.

The following spring found Beth gearing up for work in her garden. She had done well through the winter, taking on sewing classes. It was a hobby for her. One day around the end of may month, Beth got a call. Her Henry had taken a massive heart attack and died. Beth grieved for weeks although they had been divorced for a few years. He was still in her heart. The children did not seem to be to upset as he had never had much time for them. Michelle visited her mother much more often now as she was ailing a little. She thought old age was ugly. It takes your soul and leaves you as a shadow of your former self. Her mother's eighty-ninth birthday was coming up in June, so she got the siblings together to plan a party for her. As in the much younger days her mom and dad had a lot of company for parties, she knew her mother would love this.

When the day of the party arrived, the children came and so did her many grandchildren. Beth smiled and hugged every one of them and looked happy to see everyone. Her children and grandchildren were her life. She loved them more than anything. The lovely cake was served, and the gifts were also opened. The little music boxes that she so loved played along with the other voices of her children. They sang happy birthday to her with all the love that was in their hearts that day. They so loved and respected their strong mother. After some time, Michelle could see that her mother was going back in memory of them all in happier times a long time ago. Tears welled in her eyes to see the sad look in her mother's eyes. So they sang some more, and Beth loved it all. Her children are all here to celebrate my life, she thought. At about evening she was getting tired and wanted to lie down. Michelle settled her into bed. After she hugged all of her grandchildren and her own children, she thanked them all for coming and told them that she loved them.

They all said good night to her, and as she laid down her head, she had a happy smile on her face. God took her hand and brought her to a much happier place that night. That was the way her children found her the next morning—with a smile on her face. Michelle thought, *You are in heaven now, Mom, with all the beautiful angels helping you in your garden.* The funeral was a large one; it seemed the whole town turned out to be there. Michelle glanced around at the many faces of these people. She did not know most of them, but they knew that she was Beth's daughter as she looked like her mother's twin. One lady asked, "Are you Beth's daughter or her younger sister?" It was obvious that her mother was well-liked in this little town. Michelle overheard another woman say, “Poor Beth. I knew her well.”

“She was my best friend also,” said Annie. “But she had a hard life with that husband of hers taking her business and then having the nerve to cheat on the poor woman.”

Michelle watched for the lady after the funeral, and she walked up to her. She introduced herself. Annie gasped, “My lord! Young lady, you almost gave me a heart attack. Looking at you is like looking into Beth's face.”

Michelle smiled briefly. “Did you know my mother well?” she asked.

“Know her? My dear, I was her best friend for many years”—she looked away—“but then she stopped calling, and I tried, but she never seemed to have time for me anymore. Sorry, child.” she said. “My name is Annie. Come visit me soon. Jody will be there too—that's her other friend.”

Michelle was left the house in the will, and also the diary. But she could not have that until she reached sixty-four, which was in six months. It was many months later that Michelle stood in front of her mother's grave; she could not bring herself to come before. Her tears fell as she remembered the last day that they had spent with her. It was her birthday. It bothered Michelle for years now that there was something not right with her mother, as every time she called, her mother made excuses as to why she could not come to visit or for them to come to her. Michelle was the eldest daughter and carried all the responsibility of what had occurred and was to occur, as unknown to Michelle. The killer was still out there, life went on for her to struggle as best she could. She must go to visit her mother's grave again; it gave her comfort and the strength to go on.

CHAPTER TWO

Michelle stood in front of her mother's grave. Tears streamed down as she remembered the last day they had spent with their mom. It was her birthday; she was eighty-nine. Michelle was the eldest daughter, and for years now she had this feeling that something was not right in her parents' life, especially these last few years as her mother had always made up a story as to why she couldn't come to visit at certain times. She sounded happy enough, but the happy tone of her voice was not there as it used to be.

Michelle decided to do some digging as she was aware that her mom knew a lot of people around this little town. She now lived in the little house by the brook as it was left to her in the will, as was the business. It was left for all of them, but the brothers and one sister Lou wanted Michelle to buy them out as they had good careers and had no time to run it. So it was settled as Michelle loved to run it like her mom. The deer and birds were there as she drove into the yard. She sat in her mom's chair by the window in the coffee room. Tears came down as she could picture her in the garden she loved. The birds were singing on this lovely day, but Michelle felt no joy.

Her heart ached now; she cried it out and then had a nap. In the afternoon, she went to Jody's house. Jody was a good friend of her mother. Michelle asked her how her mom was the last few months before she died. Jody thought for a moment, then said, "You know, she did not go out that much anymore, never came to visit like she used to." Then she said something that caught Michelle's attention.

"Henry was so mean to her when he was alive, it's no wonder she was depressed."

Then Michelle asked Jody, "What do you mean? Were mom and dad fighting?" Jodie looked away.

"My, I have said too much already. I'm sorry, dear, but I promised your mom not to say anything."

Michelle was now very curious and very upset over this bit of information. She went home and sat for a while, but it was bugging her so much that she started wondering about mom's diary that no one was supposed to see. On the reading of the will they were told that the eldest child would inherit the private diary when she reached the age of sixty four, to which Michelle would be in a few months.

The next day she went into the city to see the lawyer. He was a reasonable man and told her she would have to sign papers to which the other children would not see this diary. Michelle did so, and a week after that, the diary was released to her. With tears of joy she went home, took the phone off, locked the doors, and settled down to reading her mother's innermost private thoughts. Somehow she felt guilty reading this as she was sure her mother was probably watching. "I am sorry, Mother," she whispered. "But I love you and want to know if things were all right with you and dad."

She opened the diary; tears fell as there were dried roses on the front page from her wedding day long ago and a picture of them when they were so very young and in love. Michelle smiled at her mother's look of joy with her long black hair short as she was and her dad, so tall. She cried, *Momma, wish you were here. I hope this is a good sign on these pages that you were happy.*

She turned the next page. There were photos of their christenings; there, as well, was a piece of paper. It looked like a legal document. Michelle opened it and began to read. It was of the day her mom opened and named her business H and B photography. Michelle was puzzled as she always knew it as B and A photograpy. *That's strange*, she thought. She put it back and turned the following pages. Just some pictures of special events and writings of stuff. It was when she read the fifth page that it caught her attention. The words were stained, like coffee or maybe like tear stains; so much so that Michelle had a hard time making it out. But a word jumped out at her like a bolt of lightning. It said betrayed something. She got the big light on it and read "Henry betrayed me today." Michelle's eyes filled with tears as she read of her dad taking the company away from her mom, and the mean way he had come to treat her.

Michelle's heart was breaking now as she read of him making her mother sign papers, or he would leave her. "Oh, poor mother!" she cried. She read of her mom trying to call her the day she ran away, and finally, how her father had tried to kill her. Michelle read these words in disbelief as she was now heartbroken, picturing her mother out on the road, trying to hide. "God!" she cried, "why was I not home that day?"

She read about the killing of Don and her dad killing himself and of her mother now in this diary, asking her many months later to forgive her for not telling Michelle the truth. "Oh, Mom," she whispered, "there is nothing to forgive. Your life was threatened." She grabbed her mom's favorite pillow and cried, brokenhearted, into it most of the night. She was also in shock as to the monster her dad must have been to do that to her mother. All night Michelle tossed and turned, picturing her mom and dad fighting and her poor mother trying to get away from this monster that had now become so in Michelle's mind. She sat up in bed, crying aloud, "Oh, Mother, why didn't you let me know? I could have been here for you!" She cried out into the night, for this had all happened before Michelle moved.

She looked at their portrait on the night stand; it seemed her mother, now knowing what she did, looked unhappy and miserable on this picture. *Funny,* Michelle thought, *it takes something like this to make a person really pay attention.* As she stared into her mother's eyes, she thought she could hear her voice.

It's all right, child, I love you.

"I love you too, Mother," Michelle said to her mom's picture. The next morning Michelle put on dark glasses to go to the library. There she looked up any hunting accidents in the older papers. Sure enough, there it was, her dad and the don guy. It was pictures of them alive, but the caption said that they had died by accident, except that the other guy committed suicide. Michelle now knew differently, but she still did not know how her dad was to kill her mom as she did not have anything in the diary about it. All of a sudden she stopped dead in her tracks. *Oh God, what if he hired someone to do it? They could still be looking for her,* thought Michelle. She hurried home to lock her doors and windows.

The next day Michelle went into the city to the police; she brought the diary with her to explain why she was asking about the threat on her mother's life. The police read the diary and said the case has been closed for years now, but as they had not had any evidence that he hired a killer. They would check to put her mind at rest to see if there was any stranger from out of province around this area of the north. But it being a small town, anyone strange here, they would know about it, and know their business.

As life went on, Michelle decided not to tell her family as it would serve no purpose. She put the diary into a safe deposit box and hid the key, hoping she would find a way of getting rid of it, so if anything happened to her, they would not find it; after all, it was now hers. As the months went on, Michelle settled into her usual routine. One day she had some trouble with her phones. It seemed that it stormed the night before, and it had gotten the phone lines all mixed up, so she called out to phone company to get it fixed.

The next day he was to come. Michelle did not like to be without a phone. The following day it was restored. As the technician was leaving, he put something on her side table; it looked like a little tape of some kind. Michelle did not see it until the following evening.

She came home from work and settled in for the night as winter was coming, and in the North, you only went out if you really had to on cold nights like this. She sat by the phone to call her sister Lou. It was then she noticed the tape. She thought the technician must have forgotten this. She put it on the table and went to bed. The next day she called the phone company to tell them they had left something there.

"No," he replied, "that was in your phone."

"Oh," she said. She took the tape and popped it into the recording machine of her phone, then went to get her coffee, not paying too much attention. She heard voices from a distance. *I don't remember turning on the TV*, she thought to herself. She went to the living room and the voices got closer. *Some boring movie*, she thought. But the TV was not on. Puzzled, Michelle went to the coffee room; the voices got closer. She stopped just inside the door to listen, for it was the tape she had put in.

Her legs turned to rubber as she grabbed at the wall to steady herself, dropping the coffee cup. The voice was her father's, saying, "Meet me on the dock by the boat at midnight."

Michelle's blood ran cold as the voice at the other end was raspy, but she could hear the words that will stay with her forever.

"Where do you want the body dumped?" it asked. Then there was silence. Michelle sank onto the couch nearby. Her heart was beating so hard she could hear it. This must have been the killer that was hired to murder her mother. *Dear God*, she thought, *what if he is still out there somewhere?* She sprang off the couch, grabbed the tape, and ran out the door. Driving like a demon, Michelle went to the police with the tape. She was in shock; they tried to calm her down, and they called Jody, her neighbor, to come and keep her company while they listened to the tape. Michelle was terrified as she now would be the one he would kill. As far as she knew, her father may have only given him her mom's address. The police listened in disbelief while trying to be professional about the whole thing as they also could not believe that Henry would be capable of doing this, for they bowled with him every week.

As the weeks went by, Michelle was cautious as to who she talked to and where she went alone. She also always checked her home before she got near the house. She had a strategy set up. She would drive halfway to her home in the lane, sit there out of sight of anyone seeing her car, and watch for a while for anything unusual. Then she would proceed home and lock her doors and windows. Jody stayed over now on a regular basis as the police would drive by to see if everything was okay. Michelle started to relax as the months wore on and nothing happened. She went out more and came home, not letting the ghosts of her poor parents ruin her life. She knew her mom would not want her to live like that.

She and Jody played hockey every evening and played cards in winter. They glanced at each other as Michelle now demanded to know if it was possible for the killer to still be looking for her mother. Jody replied, I do not know michelle, maybe the police can tell you more". The police were not sure of much detail about it as it was many years ago that all this took place but they would look into it.

One day, just before the Christmas season, Michelle received a package in the mail; it was addressed to her poor mother. She didn't make much of it as some of her friends from away maybe did not know she was deceased. So she gave it to the mailman, saying that it had no address where she could return it to.

Christmas nearing, Michelle started decorating her home by the brook. She loved it this time of year as the snow was so bright shining on the lights of her home; it was beautiful as she decorated like her mom used to—lights everywhere. One day she went into the city to stay at the home of her friend, who was giving a Christmas party. She was lonely at this party, but she stayed there as it was also lonely to go home. The next day, upon returning, she checked her mail. There was the same strange package, no mailing address. Michelle grumbled, "Those mailmen sure make mistakes. He was supposed to take this to return to sender."

Just then the mailman was passing by, and she ran out to give him the package. He looked at her in surprise. "I took it back, Michelle," he replied.

Michelle said, "But this is the exact package."

"No," he said, "look at the date."

Sure enough, it was a different date. Michelle thanked him and went inside. *May as well open it,* she thought. *At least I can do that much for Mother*. She opened it, and it was a lovely red ceramic rose, and the note read, "Hope this finds you well, but you will be as red as this rose when I get to you." And there was a red streak of bloodlike substance across the bottom of the rose.

Michelle dropped it in shock as it crashed into a million pieces on the floor, in horror she realized that there was a killer out there after all. She grabbed her purse and ran out into the yard to her car. Terror ran through her now as she realized that he could be watching her right now. The rose had shattered into a million pieces when she dropped it, so she had nothing to show the police, only the note.

At the police station, they were very busy as the Christmas season brought many different people out of the woodwork, so to speak. The city was bad for crimes at this time of the year. Michelle must have sat there for hours as she watched hookers, robbers, and drunks coming and going. Finally, someone came to her aid. By now she had calmed down enough to explain about the strange package and show them the note. They read it and checked for fingerprints, but to no avail as Michelle had handled it too much. There was nothing they could do, she was told, but to be careful, and they would look into it as soon as possible.

Michelle stayed in the city that night, for she was too terrified to go to the home that she had decorated so happily just a few days before. She slept badly that night. The next day, a constable from the police followed her home to check her house out to see if she would be okay. Nothing was amiss, but he put a patrol car across from her lane, just to make sure, but he told her that it was only for that night as they needed every car in the city. There was not a spare around. Michelle was grateful for one. At least she would get a good night's sleep. The next morning, Michelle looked out the window; the patrol car was gone. She moved away to make coffee, but not before she caught a glimpse of an old truck. It looked strange. She didn't make much of it as she started her day. *Probably someone home for Christmas*. Her doors were locked anyway, she thought. No one can get in here; it was like Fort Knox. She smiled as she recalled her friend Jody sending her husband over to put on extra locks.

As the days wore on, Michelle never forgot about the ugly incident, but she relaxed to the point of having friends over for the holiday festivities. She laughed a lot and tried to be happy. On one of these nights, she was on her way to Jody's for a party. She went early as Jody wanted help to set up for it. She arrived there and rang the bell. The puppy they had was going crazy. *That's strange*. She smiled. He was used to Michelle and never barked like that. Jody will shoo him away she smiled. She knocked on the door this time as she thought maybe her doorbell wasn't working. But as she did, the door came open, and the puppy ran past her.

"Hey!" she called. "Come back, Suzy! Jody, your dog just ran again!" There was no answer. The smell of cooking was coming from the kitchen. It smelled so good. Michelle thought, *I'll check on the food. Maybe she is in the shower*. She went into the kitchen; there was a turkey on the counter, but it looked like there was blood on the knife lying next to it. "Jody," she called, "did you hurt yourself?"

Michelle ran into the hallway, for the dog had come back and was barking to get in. "Okay, little gal," she said, "come on in." The dog leaped past her and streaked upstairs as if it was scared of something. Michelle laughed out loud. *Silly puppy*.

"Jody, your dog got spooked!" she laughed.

She ran upstairs after the dog. Maybe she was getting dressed. "That's some turkey you have, enough for an army of people."

She rounded the corner of the hallway and into Jody's room. There on the floor was her friend. Michelle screamed hysterically as she was lying there in a pool of blood, and the dog was licking it. She fell to her knees in horror as the dog ran away, and she could see the blood oozing out the side of Jody's neck. She summoned enough sense to grab the phone to call the police. They came right away, and Michelle, almost out of it from exhaustion, finally was able to go home to a lonely place, now that her friend would not be coming to stay with her anymore. She wept for her, as she thought of what the police had said. "The crazies come out in any holiday season. Maybe they knew her, or maybe there was someone looking for drugs as Jody was a nurse. They may have figured to score some."

Michelle didn't buy that story as Jody didn't keep drugs in her home for fear of that reason. The next morning, Michelle had to go to the airport to pick up husband. He was storm an bound the night of her death. He was taking the news very badly as Jodie and her husband were very close. She was like an older sister to Michelle, and Sam was like a big brother, always watching over her.

As Christmas passed, Michelle had a hard time getting over her friend's death. She and Sam went out together a lot now as they were both lonely for Jody. They took comfort in each other's company. Sam didn't want to be in that house without her, so he ended up selling it and moving to the city. Michelle continued to live her life as normally as she could. As the days went by, Michelle was getting ready for the fishing derby that was held every year in the North. Hundreds of people entered it to catch the biggest pike or whatever came out of the water. Michelle always volunteered; as did Jody. She would miss her this year.

The day of the derby arrived. The weather was cooperating for a change; it was bright, and the sun glistened on the lake. It was also very cold, but that didn't stop these people, for they were a hardy bunch. Licenses were bought, and lots of people lined up to watch. Michelle was responsible for selling the food. The traffic was busy as she had ever seen in many years. Suddenly a guy came along in an old truck. Something jogged at her memory about that old truck. It seemed familiar to her in some sense. Anyway, she forgot about it, but not the guy getting out of that old truck. He was about six foot one, two hundred pounds at least, thought Michelle. He had a gray beard and dirty headband. *Not a bad-looking guy*, mused Michelle. *One of those big, woodsy kind of guys.* He bought a sandwich, staring at her the whole time. He asked in a friendly manner if she was from around here. Michelle smiled and replied yes, that she loved the North. He looked at her once more, then walked away.

The day was long; many winners had to be announced. Finally, it was over for another year. Michelle was getting ready to leave. She noticed the old truck still there. *Maybe one of those dedicated fisher guys.* She smiled to herself. The evening was lovely as Michelle drove home. The snow was now coming down softly, and it was peaceful driving along, but still very cold. No busy traffic, so far, she thought. She hummed to the music; a car passed her, going a little too fast, she thought. She thought about Jody as the police didn't have any suspects as yet. *Probably some nut case*, Michelle thought angrily. The road had many dangerous turns and a high drop on one side of the highway where she drove now. She slowed a little now as another vehicle could not pass on this side of the road. She could see that old truck coming a little too fast for this part of the highway. *Why can't people learn to slow down?* She had to go to the other side so this maniac could pass, but he was not trying to pass.

Michelle could see him in her rearview mirror; he was following her pace, not trying to get ahead. She was now getting worried as there was no one around. You were in the middle of nowhere up north most of the time, as it depended where you traveled. Michelle now watched this guy, as when she sped up, so did he. Her thoughts were, *What is this guy trying to do?* Nervously she sped up a little to see what he would do. He did the same thing. In a little panic now, she tried calling Sam on his cell phone. There was no answer as cells didn't work this far out. Michelle drove carefully now as the drop was coming up, and she was nervous at the thought of looking there.

She drove normally; so did the driver of the truck. She signaled for him to pass, but he did not want to do that. Suddenly he started speeding toward her car and swerving a little as if he was trying to get her to speed as well. Michelle was now frightened of this man. *Oh my god,* she thought, *maybe he is the killer.* Now she was really terrified. Suddenly, he came upon her like a demon, hitting, her from behind. Terror ran through Michelle as she tried to keep the car on the road and away from the cliff. The guy came again, hitting her hard. *This is it,* thought Michelle. *He is going to kill me. Oh Lord.* She prayed in tears of terror now as he came up alongside her and tried to push her to the side of the road.

"What are you doing!" she screamed at him, but he was smiling at her in a nasty way. Michelle hit the brakes to slow down, but it was too late. As she did so, he rammed her from behind, and her car left the road going down the small cliff in a sliding speed. Horror went through her. She then lost all consciousness.

Michelle opened her eyes. For a second, she could not focus. Slowly she looked around. *Dear God, where am I?* she thought. Then she tryed to sit up in her seat; her head was bleeding profusely as was her leg. The moon was out. She looked around, trying to see where she was. She knew she was at the bottom of the cliff as she could see the highway. Then she remembered. Terror ran through her again as she thought of what happened. Her head hurt so much she could barely see. She tried to remember his face, but it was very foggy. But she would remember, in time she thought.

She could not tell how late it was, or how long she had been out of it. *Please, someone help me,* she tried to scream but her head got worse, as she did so. She looked at her leg, she had to stop the bleeding somehow. All that night, Michelle stayed awake, afraid to close her eyes, for there were wolves and other Northern animals around here. She tried to roll up the window, but it did not work as, she only got it half way. She was too afraid to move as she wasn't sure how hurt she was. She must have passed out again, for when she awoke, it was light—well, as light as it gets in the North in winter. The cold was seeping into her body now as it was at least thirty degrees below most days.

Michelle rubbed her hands together and thought about Sam. If her cell phone worked, it would help, but she knew it would not. A deer came out into the clearing to see the strange sight. It was very big, thought Michelle. She now had no feeling in her left leg. Fear went through her at the thought of freezing to death before she was found. She may never be found here. *Please let someone find me, mother,* she thought. *Please watch over me.* Then she passed out again, from the pain.

It must have been hours later when Michelle opened her eyes. It was black now as the moon was covered in a stormy haze. *Oh Lord,* she thought, *don't let it storm, not yet*. She tried to get the car door open. She was freezing. If she could reach the back seat, she had a big blanket there, as well as a first aid kit. She always brought winter emergency stuff along, as up there, you have to be prepared for anything. Reaching back as much as she could, Michelle screamed in agony as she grabbed at the blanket. The pain shot up her leg and nearly knocked her out again. She fought the weakness to keep her eyes open. *Don't go to sleep*, she now thought. *You'll never wake up*. The pain now got worse as yet another night passed. Michelle dozed, only to open her eyes again. She had to do something to stay awake. The cold was making her drowsy now. The bleeding had finally stopped on her head and leg. She was grateful to be alive but the pain was incredible.

Some animals were around; she could hear the wolves in the distance. She normally loved that sound, but not now as she was helpless in the middle of nowhere with her car window halfway down, a target for anything. Fear now ran through her as she was helpless and could not move much, only her right leg. She tried to get the window up and the motor going to get some heat. Tears fell hard as nothing seemed to work. The blanket was helping to keep her a little warm.

The next day—Michelle guessed it was another day as she could not tell, she was getting very hungry. She knew she had food and water, but it was in her trunk. She waited for a while to get the courage to get out of the vehicle. *If I don't*, she thought, *I'll for sure die here*. Slowly she lifted her good leg and tried to move. The pain shot through her, which made her cringe, but she had to move. The door opened slightly, after much pushing, and she fell out of the car half in and out. Michelle looked around in fear. *I cannot leave this vehicle*. She knew that you never leave your vehicle when in an accident in the cold north.

Finally, after an agonizing time, she finally reached the trunk. Leaning on the car, she struggled to open the broken trunk. After much time, she grabbed her little cooler, then froze in her tracks. She heard a low growl, for there in front of the car was a lone wolf/Terror now ran through her, for it smelled her blood as it was all over her. She screamed for it to leave. She half crawled, half ran to get inside. The animal stood there, growling fiercely now, as it came toward her, she managed to get inside, screaming loudly now as the pain and fear were overwhelming. The animal moved closer looking for her blood.

She locked the door, still screaming to get it to go away. Thanking God she was at least alive—but for how long, she did not know. The wolf stayed around. Michelle knew that others would now come as well. They smelled her blood; they would watch her all night. She lived long enough up north to know it was a dangerous place to live, especially in winter. You always had to be prepared in this harsh climate, for any kind of danger. Another day passed into night. Michelle was very thirsty as her rations were running low now. She prayed that someone would see the car. She must have fallen asleep, for when she awoke, the car was moving. Terror was in her body as it went stiff with fear, at what she saw. The wolves were all around the car one had a large paw halfway through her window. All of a sudden there was a blast of something; gunshots, rang in the air. "Oh God," she said to herself, "am I dreaming?" But she was not; shadows came around the car,—it was three men.

"Are you okay?" they called to her as she was in a daze now.

Michelle suddenly, screamed, "Please get me out of here!" Then she passed out. When she awoke, it was to light and warmth and sound. She could not see for a moment, but as her vision cleared, she could see Sam in the hallway of a hospital. She guessed she must have made a sound, for he, as well as her family, came rushing into the room. There were tears in their eyes as they told her that she had been missing for three days and nights. Michelle could only stare at those loving faces as she was here, alive. She was lucky, they told her as the cold and animals could have killed her. It was a week later that Michelle was well enough to go home. She told the police of the man who caused the accident, describing him as best she could. The old truck was picked up, and the man was charged for attempted murder. Michelle later learned that he had been hired by one Henry Lobee many years back. He had been paid and had to do his job, not knowing what her mother looked like. The address was the only thing given to him, but then he found her picture on his nightstand, the last time he talked to henry he must have left it for him, said the killer. It was quite a story that he told. Michelle now lives in her little house by the brook; her sister Lou now lives with her as the left leg gives her much pain, and she can't get around much anymore. Michelle is very happy that justice was done, she smiles at Sam across the coffee room. As her husband, he takes her by the hand, and they sit out on the deck and listen to the birds and watch the deer come closer for a look. They had gotten married a couple years after Jody died. The brook has a comforting sound; they laugh a lot and are very happy. Michelle is now happy in her life; everything was justified in her mother's life and in hers—so she thought;

CHAPTER THREE

Michelle was working at the company one day and decided to go home early to sort her mother's belongings. She dreaded this chore but knew it had taken her four years to get to it; now was that time—after all, it had been a long time. She went into her mothers old room to which she never used, and sat on the bed. She could picture her mother painting the walls in spring, or just making the bed. She pulled out some boxes and started sorting her clothes and shoes. It took a long time as her mom had a lot of things.

Something fell to the floor when she took a box from the shelf near the closet. It was another diary, very worn-looking, and it had colors on it like a young person's would have. It said, "My Teen Years: Very Private." Michelle giggled. She thought this must be her very young years. She opened it and, with a smile, began to read. She smiled through all the pages as they described every boy that her mom had met. Michelle laid it aside to go for her coffee. Later she came back to the diary. It was a old diary, but she wanted to really know what her mom was like as a very young teen. It went on to say how school was an airy, big old schoolroom and that a potbellied black stove stood in the middle of the classroom, how they would be so cold waiting for the teacher to light it, and how they kept their coats and mittens on until it got warm. Michelle laughed out loud at some of the stories. Her mom, it seemed, was very popular with the opposite sex to.

Michelle was proud of her mom. She was a great person. She turned the page, still smiling. Then her smile started to fade as she read on. This was very serious stuff her mother had put in here now. Her eyes widened as she read on. Her mother had turned nineteen on August seventeenth and had a party with her friends, Michelle read. That night, as she was walking home from the party, alone as her friends did not want to leave as yet, she was dragged into a corner by the church and beaten. Michelle started to weep as she pictured her poor young mom fighting off a person on her birthday. Tears of sorrow fell for her mom. She read on, through her tears, of them finding out it was one of her classmates who committed this crime, as he was mentally challenged and it was hidden from the public as in those days a person didn't speak of these things—you just suffered.

Anger shot through Michelle as she thought how much this woman had endured in her lifetime. She read how angry her mom was as she suffered in silence, how her father tried to do the same, "one night in his drunken state, He hated me," her mom had written. "Even as I got older, I started standing up to him, and his revenge was to try and kill me and abuse me for that reason. I ran away that night." *My god*, thought Michelle as tears rolled down onto the pages. What a horrible life her mother had endured; the audacity of someone hurting a woman in so many ways, no respect for her as a human being. Michelle laid the book aside now and wept a little more. *I will destroy this*, she thought, *as I'm sure mother would not want this known*. Her honor was to this sad woman who had suffered a life of hardships and now was at peace. *I love you, Mom. I'll keep your secrets for you in my heart forever*. She put the diary in the fire and watched the clean flames take it away. It felt right to do this as it seemed her mother was cleansed by it now and finally at peace, so was the daughter who loved her so much. This chapter in my life is now closed. *Good-bye, Mother. Rest in peace in love in beauty in heaven.*

Michelle went on to live her life. As time passed, she was happier. One day a lovely daughter came to her and she was fulfilled, for they had adopted a little girl but was a long time waiting for her arrival. She called her Lisa Beth. When Lisa was ten, she came running into the kitchen.

"Mom," she cried, "there is a man out there in the bush, watching me."

Michelle instantly locked all doors and windows. She peeked outside, and sure enough, there was a man standing there, staring at the house. Michelle thought he looked familiar. "Lisa, you take the dog and go to your room and lock the door. Don't open it for any reason except when I come to get you."

"Okay, Mom," Lisa said.

Michelle called the police. They were concerned as the prison had two men escape a couple of days ago. They informed Michelle of this. She could feel the old fear coming back as she remembered the guy who tried to kill her. The police came and checked around. The man had disappeared, they informed her. Michelle went to get her daughter from her room. That following night was a sleepless one for Michelle as she kept peeking out her windows looking for that man. *Oh God*, she thought, *don't let it be him, maybe just some person wanting to break in for food.* The next day, Michelle and her daughter went into the city to shop. They had lunch with a friend and bought clothes and shoes and had a lot of fun. It was Saturday, so it was good to take her mind off Friday's upsetting events. They drove home in a happier mood, and Lisa fell asleep.

Michelle smiled on her lovely daughter. She was so lucky, she thought. She and Sam and Lisa were a happy family. If only mother could see them. Now she guessed that mother was watching them and protecting them also. She drove into the yard; the flowers were looking lovely in the dusky evening. There were lilies as white as the snow, and the gurgling of the brook. It was peaceful to hear. The roses were a faded red winter was here. The whole evening looked wonderful and serene but cold.

Michelle said to Lisa, "Come on, sleepyhead, we are home." She awoke with a start.

"How come Buddy is not greeting us?" she asked. Michelle thought. *That is strange.* Buddy usually barked a greeting when they came into the yard.

"Oh, he is probably being a sleepy head also," she replied. They both laughed at this. She unlocked the back door, as it was closer to the kitchen. "Buddy!" she called. There was no answer. Suddenly Lisa screamed from the kitchen area. Michelle dropped the packages and ran into the kitchen. There on the floor lay Buddy. He looked sick, and blood was coming out of his mouth. "Momma," Lisa cried, "do something!" Michelle ran to the phone and called the police and told them what happened. They were on the way, they said, with a vet.

They wrapped the puppy in a warm blanket; Lisa was sobbing. *Did he get into any cleaners?* Michelle thought. *Maybe I better check.* She comforted her daughter, reassuring her that Buddy was going to be okay. Then she checked the cleaners. There was nothing amiss. The police arrived with the vet, who immediately went to examine the dog. He came back in a while to inform Michelle that the dog had been poisoned. Michelle looked at him in shock.

"Poisoned!" she replied. "But he was inside the whole time we were gone today."

"Did you lock all of your doors?" the police asked her. "Yes, I did," replied Michelle. A few minutes later, the police came back to Michelle.

"May I speak to you alone?" he asked. Michelle followed him out to the back door.

"Your home has been broken into," he said, pointing out the broken lock on the front door. Michelle's heart came up into her throat.

"You mean someone broke in here and poisoned our dog?"

"Yes, it looks like that's what happened." He started to write up his report. Michelle was in tears of fright now.

"Do you think he might be still out there?"

"I don't want to scare you, but it's a possibility," replied the police. She asked if he could get a locksmith out to replace the broken one. Not until tomorrow, they said. The police advised her to stay at a friend's house for tonight. Meanwhile, they would keep an eye on the house and send a patrol car out. Michelle called her mom's best friend Annie and explained the situation. Annie was very concerned and said, "Come right away."

They arrived at Annie's home later in the evening. She welcomed them with warmth and concern for Lisa and her poor puppy. Lisa cried, they finally got her settled in bed and then they settled down for the night. Michelle and Annie sat for hours talking about the day's unfortunate events. She suddenly had tears streaming down her face.

"What is it, child?" Annie asked. "It's going to be okay, you know."

"It's not just that," Michelle replied. "What if it's the guy who tried to kill my mom, and then tried to kill me?" She then proceeded to tell Annie of the prison break.

"Oh my god!" Annie exclaimed. She rushed around the house, locking doors and windows. Annie also had an alarm system, so if anyone came near her home, the police would be right there. She assured Michelle of this, and Michelle settled down a bit.

The next morning, they had a lovely breakfast with Annie, telling jokes to lighten things up. They laughed and were happy to know the dog was going to live. The vet had called early to let Lisa know this. She was a happy child once again. The following day Michelle went to the business, then they went into town again to shop.

Michelle and Lisa went home to find a locksmith there, fixing the door.

He said, "I put a new, stronger lock on here as the old one was very weak."

Michelle then decided to get all of her locks put on new. They settled down for the day as Lisa had school the following day. The dog was brought back home in good health, and her daughter was once again very happy. She put her daughter and the dog to bed and settled in for the evening. She went outside and sat in her mom's chair and watched the little brook and viewed her lovely garden, that had faded away to a few colorful twigs. Her mother worked very hard in this beautiful garden. *Oh, Mother, I wish you were still here.* She stared at the garden for a moment, picturing her mom there. She could almost see her planting her favorite roses and her lilies, and she smiled at this one—the man in the bush plants. They were trees that spread all over and bloomed through to September; burgundy-colored flowers bloomed on them and her hostas. She smiled more now. Her mom loved hostas. They grew very large for her mom, but Michelle could never get them to grow bigger. Tears ran down her face while thinking of all of her mom's sayings and seeing her in the garden by the brook. Michelle felt a peacefulness suddenly come over her. She then knew then that her mother was still in this garden with her. She went inside. *Good night, Momma, love you always.* She felt happier than she had in a long time.

Life went on as usual. She was relaxed a little now as there was no more news about this killer. She was now getting ready for Halloween. She decorated the deck and all her doors for her daughter. They were planning a Halloween party for the neighborhood—a big one, as Lisa called it. Plans were put in action; the women were cooking and baking Halloween cookies and all kinds of stuff. Michelle did some also, but was busy putting out fliers for the party. The garden looked lovely with some flowers left. The hardier ones didn't go until the end of fall. It was a lovely glow of lights—amber and reds and oranges ran along the deck, and the backyard was all aglow with colored lights. It looked spectacular, Michelle was thinking. *Oh, mother, hope you can see this, for this is as much for you as for anybody.*

CHAPTER FOUR

AUDACITY TO SURVIVE

Michelle woke up the next morning, looking forward to the Halloween party that evening, and hoping everybody showed up. The baking was done, and things were all set to go. She was very happy as she got treats ready for the children who would be coming after school at four. Sure enough, the parents were coming in droves with their little pumpkins and witches and spidermen. Michelle had dressed like a friendly witch as to not scare the children. After a few hours, it was all done for the children, except now the bigger kids came—but not too many of those. Michelle drew a sigh of relief as the last child left. She still had plenty of treats to give out, but it would be used at the adult party. *I may as well get dressed up a little more,* she thought. Just as she headed upstairs, the doorbell rang again. She smiled. *Oh, one more is not going to hurt.* She opened the door.

There on the step was a box. There was no one around. Michelle picked it up and took it inside. *Strange*, she thought, *no treats but a trick*. She smiled as she opened the small box.

Her blood ran cold as she looked at what was inside. It was a picture of her when she was about Lisa's age it was her mothers picture. There was also a bloody knife with a note that said, "Trick or treat, trick or treat, I'm going to make you bleed." The box fell from her hands as the terror she felt before returned. *Please keep my daughter safe*, she thought. It was the man outside of the house that day; it was the man who escaped. Now he was out there, waiting to kill her.

"Oh god!" she screamed.

She was all alone right now, and he was out there. She ran and grabbed the phone, called the police and then Annie to tell her to keep Lisa there if she came to her house for treats. Annie wanted to know all about it, but Michelle said, "I will tell you later."

The police arrived, took the box and its contents, and wanted Michelle to go with them, but the invitations were sent out for the party. People were arriving, looking with curiosity at the police. Michelle put on a smiling face.

"Oh, he just looks like a policeman," she said. "They were leaving, they were looking for treats." She laughed. She was safe now as everybody was here; the music played, and everyone was having a great time. Around midnight, they started to wander home. Michelle was glad they had a good time; she did not, but no one knew it as she sang and danced with the rest of them. The last good night said, Michelle rushed around. She locked all doors and windows and left all the lights on. She then called Annie to come over with Lisa and to bring a gun. Annie gasped at what she said.

Michelle said, "Please bring it as I got a nasty trick tonight. I will tell you all about it when you get here. Please hurry."

"On my way," Annie replied. Michelle's husband was away in the service and she could not get hold of him, so Annie would spend the night. Annie and Lisa arrived a half hour later. Michelle wished she talk her husband, but there was no cell phone service up where he was. Her thoughts were scattered.

The women settled on the couch after getting Lisa to bed. Michelle had been running around, nervously locking windows and doors. The patrol car was parked a little way out by the tree. That way, if someone came to the door, they would see them.

Annie was very scared at the strange developments over these past few months. She thought to herself, *This man is not going to stop until he gets to this woman. God, let it end soon, and let them capture this person.* She knew all about the husband putting out a contract on Michelle's mother. It was a frightening experience, but that poor woman didn't even know much about it. At least her daughter knows now. They stayed up most of the night, hoping the police would catch this man coming around. But night faded into dawn; that's when the ladies went to sleep. They awoke to the dog barking; something was making him really excited. Michelle jumped off the bed to look outside. When she did so, she came face-to-face with a dirty, bearded man staring in the window. She screamed at the top of her lungs. Annie was there with a flash, gun in her hand, running to the window. There was no one there. Michelle was sobbing on the floor, not making any sense now as the shock of this was too much. Annie grabbed Lisa, who had ran out to her mother, scared of the noise, of her mothers screams, was sitting with her mother, Annie got Lisa and Michelle and got them into her car. "We are going to my home," she said. "Then we will decide what to do."

They drove for a while, then Michelle started to calm down. "What are we going to do? The police can only stay on my property 'til dawn," she said. "After that, we are not protected."

"You and Lisa will stay with me up at our cabin," Annie replied. "It's the weekend, and my husband is coming back today."

Michelle felt less tension on hearing this news. *They would be safe there*, she thought. Annie had a well-built large cabin up by the lake. If necessary, they would stay for a while there.

The lake was a clear mirror that morning as they drove along the shore. "Beautiful" was a tame way to describe this area of the North. "Paradise" was the way Annie described it; she had been coming here for years. The tall trees, the mirrored lake topped off with rays of sunshine, all made for an artist's palette. The cabin came into view; it was a Victorian-built cabin with tall brick gates, a lioness on one side and the king lion on the other side of the entrance, Annie liked her special touches. The spiraling driveway was lovely to see with flowers on both sides as you drove along the borders. Some flowers were so big, you had to strain to actually see the cabin, but they were fading now as winter was coming. "I would call this a palace," Lisa said. They all laughed. It was good to see this, thought Annie, for she knew the worst was yet to come into this family's life. She hoped not, but she knew this killers history for she had read and seen on the news about this man from way back in Michelle's mom's days, when Michelle was a little one.

They were all very happy to see Harry, Annies new husband. He had food prepared, and the fire going; the place was warm and cozy. Michelle settled Lisa down to lunch and then went to shower; they enjoyed the rest of the day sitting by the fire and telling stories. Harry went outside to get more firewood. He came back with a surprise for Lisa. He had found a kitty the day before they arrived, so Lisa had another pet to take home. They laughed all evening and had a lovely night together. Michelle was happy to be away from town and safe for a while. They all agreed. Annie said, "Maybe they will get those guys before we go back." But she assured Michelle that if she wanted to stay at the cabin longer, it would be all right for her to do so for she take care of Lisa for a few days; she would see that she got to school and all. Michelle said maybe, but for now it was great to have a man around the house.

She missed Sam, her husband, who was shipped away on duty. She had told him of the prison break and what had happened, but she didn't want to worry him as he would get in an accident or something, as his duties were dangerous enough as it was.

Harry was a good friend of Michelle's dad; they bowled together and had lots of hunting trips. It was a shock to him when died, but he thought that life must go on, especially for Michelle and Lisa.

They had a lovely weekend, and then it was time to go back. Annie and Michelle had stayed up late the night before, talking about her staying longer as she had lots of staff to run the business. So it was set; Annie would take Lisa for a few more days, and Michelle would stay at the cabin for a while. She was safe there, and Annie would call every day. Lisa understood that her mom wanted to stay longer but was worried about her being by herself. Michelle assured her that she would call her every night before bedtime. They said their good-byes and left. Michelle wandered around the cabin, looking at the lovely view. She stretched her arms out, as if to enfold this beauty before her. The deck was surrounded with the fading flowers on the back en masse. Harry and Annie had put a lot of time and love into this place. They were planning on retiring someday and settling down in the cabin by the lake.

She made a tea and settled outside on a French sofa. It was so comfortable that she must have dozed off, for when she awoke, it was dusk already. The view was breathtaking as Michelle looked around. The tall trees were almost golden in the setting sun, the flowers had some colors still blooming as never before, and the splendor was picture-perfect for an artist to paint. *Hey*, thought Michelle, *maybe I should paint this*. She giggled to herself. *Where would I find the time?* She went inside to get some food, then tried to call her husband. No answer so she left a messege. She tried calling Annie, but they were still en route to home. She went back outside to enjoy this beautiful but chilly evening some more.

The next morning, Michelle went for a leisurely walk. She had not done that in a while. She walked around the grounds, admiring the paradise she was in. A squirrel popped out of a tree. The sun was shining so brilliantly that Michelle jumped at not seeing the animal sooner. It went up the tree and came down again. Michelle stood very still so as not to scare it away. The birds were chirping away, and it seemed all animal life was awake. She sat on a bench and thought about the turn of events since that prison break. If only there was some way she could talk to this man and tell him she is not the one in the picture, but she looked so much like her mother that it was uncanny but he would kill her anyway she thought.

She mused, he must have gotten paid a lot of money to be still trying to carry out this contract on her poor mother. Michelle was glad that her mom didn't know about this.

Her stomach knotted in thinking that he was out there somewhere, waiting. She went back to the cabin and called Annie and to check on Lisa. Everything was a-okay, said Annie. Lisa was still in school. She told Michelle that she drove by her house today and there was no sign of anyone. Michelle thanked her and decided to call the police to inquire if they had arrested anyone pertaining to the prison break. They did not see anyone near her home and they were still at large. She hung up and started prancing, a little worried as to where this man, or men could be.

Little did she know that he had followed them to the lake. He had hung around Michelle's property for two days. He knew the patrol car was there, as he hid in her shed. He had broken the lock as Michelle had no reason to use the shed; she would not go there. Her husband had all of his hunting gear in there, so the contract killer outfitted himself with his equipment. He nastily laughed. This broad was going to die at the hands of her own husband. The police would connect it all to him since it was his gun and his bullets and knife. He had choices now on how to kill her. Michelle settled down a little, feeling safe out here. She made dinner and then went for another walk. The evening was getting cloudy, and chilly now, as the sun had gone down early, it meant a rainstorm, or worse//.

The killer's name was Wayne ronald clum. He had wired Michelle's phone the night he broke into her house, and the dog got his too, he recalled with an ugly scowl. He had to know when the husband was coming home so he could do the job as he would get the blame. He thought, *Two for the price of one*. He had this plan to commit the crime, and then the police would think the husband was mentally ill from his stint in the military. It was the perfect plan. He laughed to himself now as he laid on a pile of blankets.

Michelle sat in front of the large front window and watched the dark clouds rolling in; it was going to be a nasty storm as even now the tall trees were swaying in the wind. Later in the evening, she tried to read some, but instead she listened to the thunder and lightning. It was getting worse. *I hope the generator holds up*, she thought. Harry and Annie were waiting for harrys retirment. That's why they were not living there yet. They were going to live out here on retirement. It was very lovely here. Michelle smiled. They were a lucky couple. She was happy that Annie had found Harry as she seemed lonely when michelle became friends with her, after her moms funeral.

Later that night, Michelle was awakened from a sound sleep by a cracking noise. She jumped out of bed and ran to the window. There was a tree split in half from the lightning. She thanked God it didn't fall on the cabin; instead, the other half lay on the ground. She looked on the other side of the house, and it looked awful. Branches were everywhere, and some flowers were damaged from the debris from this storm. Michelle called Annie. There was no dial tone. *Oh my*, she thought, *now I'm really in trouble, No phone.* But Annie knew there was a storm up there, as she heard it on the news. Michelle settled down for the day, looking out at the wind. She wanted to go for a walk, but not yet, she thought.

Wayne ronald was near the cabin. He spent the night in the back guesthouse now as it was storming really bad, he was glad he had a roof over his head, or else he would have had to do the job tonight, just to have somewhere to stay. He smiled with a sneer on his face, as he thought of his plans. He had a good night as he watched the cabin and the storm. He even managed to find food there. He thought it would be so easy now to do the job, but he had other plans. In this man's sick mentality, he was proud of his occupation as a contract killer.

He killed his first victim at the age of fourteen. His parents were abusive alcoholics who didn't care if he was around or not. They had their own misery, as his mother ran away with another man so he ran away from them at the age of twelve. One night, his drunken father beat him with a leather strap and then tried to sexually abuse him, so he left and never looked back after trying to kill him. They didn't report him missing because no one looked for him. So be it, he thought bitterly. Even now it hurt and angered him, and so to the city streets he came and learned all the bad things that was there. He also learned to survive; it was dog-eat-dog, and if you weren't part of a group, you were beaten and sometimes even killed. He joined a gang very quickly just to survive. Drugs were also part of his young life. He sold it and used it to keep from facing the total misery that his life had become. Wayne ronald was thinking about all these as he drove his old pickup out from behind the shed, *You are alive, lady, only because of your old man*, he thought as he drove away.

Michelle thought she heard a motor running somewhere, but she assumed that it was a hunter or something. She settled down to a nice dinner and waited to see if the wind would die down. She wanted to go for a walk. She loved to walk after a rainstorm, to smell the freshness of nature.

Lisa was missing her mother, so she called her number. There was no answer. "Aunt Annie!" she cried. "My mom is not answering the phone." Annie looked at her worried face.

"It's okay, honey," she said. "There was a bad storm there last night, and the phones are out, but I know your mom is all right."

Lisa was still worried. "May we go up tomorrow?" she asked. "Of course," Annie replied, "your mother may come back tomorrow."

The day dragged on now for Michelle. She was not looking forward to tonight as she would be in darkness except for the outside light of the moon that she could see peeking out from the clouds. It was clearing up. She was happier, but now it was getting too dark to go for a walk. She was more worried about bears, as with no lighting they tended to break into cabins to get food. She was not sure when they went into hybernation. Michelle also knew that with these large windows, they could easily break them. Annie had told her several years ago that harry had told her that a bear came right up to the window and pawed to get in, but he had a rifle then and it was in summer. Michelle, however, wouldn't know how to use one. She quickly looked for a candle, for it was going to be a long night.

Things seemed Eerie in the candlelight, but it was beautiful also. Michelle could see her reflection in the windows, and the lighting gave the room a warmth and beauty that only made the outdoors more attractive. The moon was bright now, but it was still a little cloudy. As the night went on, Michelle gazed out at the tall trees, and the lake was like a lovely big mirror. It was a romantic night, thought Michelle, thinking about her husband, Sam. He would love this setting. All of a sudden Michelle caught something move in the shadows. There were many shadows as the moon kept going in and out behind a cloud that was hanging around. The movement was rustling the bushes nearby now as it moved closer to the cabin. Michelle was a little nervous, but the doors were strong and the windows were locked.

She went quickly into the kitchen to get something to make a loud noise. They say that if it's a bear, to make noise, and they would be scared away. She grabbed pots and pans and ran back to see where it was. But the rustling in the bushes had stopped. Michelle looked anxiously toward the doors, hoping it wasn't outside. After an hour or so, she must have fallen to sleep, for when she awakened there was a bright big moon shining right on her in the room. She smiled for a moment, but it froze. As she looked toward the window, there was the large face of a bear looking right at her and growling fiercely and pawing the window. She screamed in terror as she grabbed for the pots and pans, screaming and banging them together. She kept on doing that while screaming, “Go away! Go away!”

Finally, the animal stopped pawing the windows. It stayed there for quite some time, but it had moved away from the windows. Michelle was hoarse and exhausted over this now. She thought, *I can’t do this anymore—let things go as they may*. She felt herself fall hard to the floor in a faint. It was sometime late when she came to herself. It was daylight, and there was no sign of the bear. *Did I dream this?* she thought. But upon looking by her side, there were pots and pans lying on the floor, and there were paw marks on the windows. Thank you, God, for protecting me through this night. With that, she crawled onto the couch and was instantly fast asleep.

Annie kept Lisa home to go see her mother. She hoped things were okay when they arrived as there was no help in an emergency up there unless you had a vehicle to get to the first aid station, which was five miles away.

They drove a little faster than ordinary today as Michelle was up there two days without contact, and the storm didn’t help matters. Up there you were always in danger unless you were prepared for everything and anything in the bush.

Michelle finally awoke to a lovely, bright morning. *Oh my*. She smiled. *Isn’t this beautiful?* But she won’t take a walk today she thought, as the events from last night were still fresh in her mind, and the animal was probably still nearby.

Harry, Annie and Lisa pulled into the yard. The sight that they saw was unbelievable—trees down everywhere, flowers wrecked. They jumped out of the car. “Michelle! Michelle, are you okay?” they cried out.

Michelle heard them and came running from the back deck. “Oh! Am I ever glad to see you!” she cried. “You will not believe what I’ve been going through this past couple of days.”

“I can imagine,” replied Annie. “With the storm and all.” Michelle then gave them all a big hug, and Lisa never left her side as she recounted the story about the bear and what she did to get it to go away. Annie commented, its funny they should not be around this time of year.

All was well now as Michelle was settled at home with her daughter. The police only now sent a patrol car out every other night as there was an assumption that the prison break criminals had moved on somewhere else. The town was all no longer abuzz about it. Michelle relaxed more each day now as she tried to put it all behind her. The guy must have given up, she thought. After all, he had his money.

But she didn't know the mind of a contract killer; they keep going until the job is done, and they die or he does. That's the only way it ends, even if they are in prison or encaged somewhere. It is a burning mission to do the job. Why? Because they enjoy the challenge, and the killing becomes a part of them, like eating to stay alive. The ordinary person will entertain themselves with other activities, but a killer lives to destroy. It's a sick mind-set.

Life went on as usual. Michelle ran the business, and Lisa had her eleventh birthday party. Annie came to visit more often. Michelle's husband, Sam, was supposed to come home. He was on leave for a few weeks. Michelle was all excited preparing for a party for him as a surprise. She and Lisa shopped for it all day. Michelle was busy but a little tired now, so she went to lie down in the afternoon. She awoke sometime later and talked to Sam, then helped Lisa with her schoolwork.

Wayne ronald, meanwhile, was sitting not far away and had listened to her conversation and heard the profanity that was bestowed on him by Michelle's husband. There was a murderous look in his eyes. "Yes," he growled, "you will pay for that."

He went out of hiding and went back to his hotel on the outskirts and put on his fake beard so nobody would recognize him.

He set up his equipment and set it on the table. "This party would be a surprise all right." He chuckled nastily. "One they would not forget."

Michelle sat and gazed at her mother's portrait. She was saddened every time she thought of the terrible life she lived, but she was with the angels now. She whispered, "I love you, Momma. Good night."

The preparations for the party were underway. Annie had done some baking, and Michelle had decorated the house. She and Lisa were very excited for Sam to be coming home at last. He was to arrive the next afternoon. Michelle had several conversations with Sam over these past few days. She was telling him other news about Wayne ronald. Sam was a little worried about his family, so he personally called the police to see if the guy was arrested or not. They said they were assuming that he had left town, as there was no sign of seeing any strangers around the town. It was a close-knit town; everybody knew each other, and strangers would stick out like a beacon. Plus, everyone knew each other's business. If you started a rumor, within one hour the whole town would know about it. Michelle had no idea that her husband was in danger. She missed him so much, and so did Lisa. She was beginning to feel more secure these days. She slept better and was more active and going out to different occasions and getting more involved in community events. Little did she know that the killer was about to take her husband out. Finally, the big day arrived. Michelle and Lisa drove to the airport to pick Sam up. It was a tearful reunion as all the bad times were gone now. Sam was home for a long stretch.

They arrived home to music from the little town and band and ribbons—a hero's welcome, for most of the townspeople knew Sam and loved their own. Michelle had everything ready; most people were already inside her home. "Surprise!" they sang out when Sam entered his home.

The party went on for a long time. There were well-wishers and welcoming banners all around the town. The little garden by the brook was all alight with amber and different colors. It was a tradition in this town that for any special event, the whole town decorated to welcome the people. It was something to see—the love, the caring, and the sharing. Wayne ronald clum stood behind the corner of a big oak tree not far from Michelle's home, watching these events take place. There was anger in his eyes, but there was also something else—tears, for as a boy he had never had a birthday party or anything to celebrate his life, or any love, this was new to watch this love all around.

He angrily wiped away the tears and watched as the music played and people danced the night away. *It will be my turn now*, he thought. *I'll give them a party my style.* He laughed to himself and went on his way. Sam was overwhelmed with all the festivities that were going on just for him. He missed all this. He often told his buddies about the love and care in this little town—the hardworking people who didn't have much but would give you the last morsel of food or even the clothes off their backs. Hospitality was a natural trait for these people, and anybody who was lucky enough to be able to come here came back with a whole new perspective on life in general. Many made fun of their customs, but in the end it was known to be a way of life for others to laugh. There was ignorance in not understanding these people, but once you got to know even one of them, that changed.

The next day saw Michelle, Sam, and Lisa cleaning up after the party. Annie had come by to help; they had a few laughs over last night's events, and after had coffee on the deck. Sam looked around at the little garden by the brook. It was late October, but it still looked lovely with the trees changing colors and some flowers still blooming. He smiled to himself. *This is what I'm fighting for*, he thought. *To be able to do this, freedom of my country, freedom to have my kids go to school, freedom to live life in peace.*

The days turned into weeks, and Sam and his buddies were talking about doing some hunting before his leave was up.

This was also a tradition of these people—in summer it was fishing; in fall and winter it was hunting for meat for the winter. Moose was a staple for these people, as well as caribou and rabbit. They canned these items also. They were hardy people and very hardworking, they cut their wood in the fall and had it ready for the winter's cold, frosty nights, for living north, there were some very nasty snow and windstorms. The whole little town was almost invisible at times except for the lights that lit the streets.

"Honey," Sam inquired, "was there a break-in?" Michelle looked at him blankly.

"I told you already about the break-in."

Sam replied, "You didn't tell me about the shed."

Michelle stared at him. She said, "I don't think there was one, or the police would have told me."

"Well, all of my hunting gear is missing, and my rifle and knives," replied Sam. "I just checked, and it's all gone."

Michelle ran to the shed with Sam close behind. She looked around. "Oh my god!" she gasped. "I didn't know about this, it must have happened while I was at the cabin."

Sam replied, "We have to call the police." Michelle picked up the phone. The officer came, looked around, and checked for prints. There was none. "Whoever it was covered their tracks well." he surmised.

Sam had a list of items for him to follow up on. "Hmm," the officer said, "looks like someone wants to hunt also." Sam didn't find this funny.

The officer said, "We will look into this for you, Sam." Michelle had a sudden thought. She turned white as a ghost.

"God, what if it was that man—"

The officer looked at her gravely. He replied, "Let's hope that's not the case, ma'am."

The following week, Sam went to the city to purchase items for his hunting; they had a tradition. The whole family would go to Annie's cabin and stay there while Sam and his friends hunted. The men would come back every other night to sleep there, and Michelle and Lisa would be there with Sam. It was a family affair, so to speak. Annie and Harry would sometimes go up on the weekends, and they played cards or whatever was fun to do—have big cookouts on the nicer days, for it was getting colder now in the northern part of the country, as winter was setting in.

The following day, they started packing for the trip up to the cabin. It was a crispy, lovely, colorful kind of chilly morning. Everybody was looking forward to getting away from town for a while.

They set off the next morning. It was a lovely morning, the animals were out in droves, and the leaves had turned all colors of nature's splendor. Michelle smiled happily to herself. *It's a great day to be alive.* Sam had to stop along the way to make a phone call. Michelle wondered why he had not done this at home, but Sam said it was to remind his friends to bring extra bullets. Michelle was hoping they would get some meat this year as last time it didn't go so well. They only got a little for winter.

They arrived at the cabin. It was spectacular up there this time of year. The tall trees were looking lovely—they had turned orange and brown, and the others were a reddish hue to them. Michelle thought happily, *I'll get lots of pictures here.* She loved to do scrapbooking in her spare time. The men carried in the supplies, and Michelle and Lisa went on to put everything away. Lisa wanted to look for some squirrels and rabbits here. She loved to take photos for her class to do projects.

Sam and his friends had breakfast and then set out for a look around to plan where they were to hunt. There was lots of walking to get there. They would be back by noon, he said.

Michelle was hanging their clothes in the closet. She was smiling. It was so nice to have Sam home for a while, as he had asked for an extended leave to look after his family. She missed him a lot and wished his stint was over, but that wasn't until next year. Then he would be done for a long while. *It will be for good*, she thought. *We will be a real family again.* Something fell out of Sam's pocket; it fell on Michelle's foot. She picked it up. It was a photo of a woman—a small picture and kind of worn-looking. Michelle looked closely at it and wondered who this could be and why it was in Sam's pocket. *Maybe some relative*, Michelle thought. But she would ask him about it later.

The day wore on; the guys came back at around noon, and they had it all planned out where they would go to hunt. Michelle had dinner ready, and they ate then decided to go for a walk. She had the photo in her pocket.

"Sam," she said, "this fell out of your pocket this morning." She showed him the photo. Sam got a guarded look on his face.

"Oh!" he laughed. "That's my friend Elaine. She works with me on-site."

"Oh," Michelle replied, "why do you have her photo?"

Sam smiled. "She must have slipped it in my coat before I left. She's just a good friend."

Michelle smiled and replied, "She is very pretty." Sam hugged Michelle and replied, "Not as pretty as you but he was feeling guilty and stupid to have left the photo in his pocket, as he had, had an affair some time ago with this woman on base, but broke it of sometime ago. He hoped that it would not become known to his wife as he was lonely and stupid, and did not want to lose the woman he loved."

Wayne ronald had driven a long way back behind this family. He knew who was in the vehicles, for there were two that were used to drive the people up to the bush. He watched as they unloaded the vehicles and counted the men. There were four of them and two women—well, one and a girl. He thought to himself, *I have to find somewhere to stay for a while.*

Having a walk, Michelle, and Lisa decided to take photos of the animals that were nearby; they were having a great day together. She thought to herself, *It's good because we don't get enough quality time together.* They went back to the house to make lunch.

The guys were having a nice day looking around to set up an outdoor camp to hunt. They were a long way from the cabin, but Michelle had a mobile phone to reach Sam if there was any problem.

Suddenly there was a knock on the door. Michelle thought, *Who would be knocking on a door in the bush and in a cabin at that?* She opened the door to a strange-looking man.

"Good afternoon," he said, "are you the lady of the house?"

"Yes, I am," replied Michelle. She noticed he had a twitch in his left eye, probably from an injury.

The man said, "I'm a hunter and just arrived up here, and my friend was supposed to leave me the keys to his place, but now I can't get hold of him—been trying all day—is it possible that you might have a spare room that I could rent for a night or so?"

Michelle thought quickly. *Should I call Sam? No.*

"All right, would you please come in. I have to call my friend, the one who owns this place, and I'll ask her if you can rent the little guesthouse. It is small but nice—only one room and kitchen and bath."

"Oh, that sounds good," the man replied with a smile.

"Okay," Michelle replied. She called Annie.

Annie said, "Yes, it is all ready."

"Yes," Michelle told the man, "she says you can rent it."

"All right, ma'am," he replied again with a smile.

"I'll get the keys, and we will go there for some paperwork," Michelle replied.

"Sure thing," the man said. They reached the little guesthouse, and it was as Annie said—ready for rent.

Michelle said, "You have to fill out this paper for my friend."

The man filled it out; she thanked him and left the cabin. She went back to her place and settled down to read the form. His name was Wayne turner. *Hmm,* Michelle thought, *nice name.* He seemed like a good person but wayne ronald did not put his real last name there.

Wayne ronald Clum drove back into town to get supplies. He chuckled nastily to himself. *That was too easy.* He was now situated where he could take any of these people out, and that broad was going to be first, for he had taken an instant dislike to Michelle; killing her after taking so long seemed very exciting to this man.

Sam called Michelle awhile later in the afternoon. She told him about the man who rented the guesthouse. Sam was wary; he asked if Annie had approved this, and if he seemed okay. Michelle replied, "Of course he seemed nice." She wasn't worried about him being close by; it would be some company for her and Lisa when Sam was out hunting

The following week, Michelle asked Wayne to supper as Sam was coming home tonight. He replied that he would be delighted, so it was set.

He was curious to get a look at the husband, as at the party he did not get a good look at him and seeing that they were the same build, he wanted to see what he was up against in this man. Michelle had a lovely supper ready when he arrived.

"Umm, smells good here," he commented.

"Yes," said Sam, who came out of the adjoining room. "Michelle is a great cook." He gave her a smile.

Oh boy, thought Wayne, *this is one of those lovey, dovey kind of relationships.* Sam shook his hand and offered him a drink, but he refused. *Have to keep a straight thought,* he said to himself, *the job has to be done soon. I need to get out of here to my next job.* He had gotten a call before he came to the bush.

Wayne had his meal then excused himself and went to leave. "Oh, by the way," he said to Sam, "when are you going out again?"

"Maybe next few days," replied Sam, "may I ask why?"

Wayne smiled. "Guess your wife didn't mention I hunt also."

"Oh, well then, I'll let you know when we go again," replied Sam. At that, Wayne took his leave.

The following few days Sam announced they were going again to hunt. "Better let our neighbor-renter know," said Michelle. "He seems very happy to hunt."

"Okay," replied Sam. "Wish us luck." Michelle did just that.

The following day, they set out on the trail. Wayne was thinking, *There are four of them. There will be a way to get to Michelle later. Now all I have to do is make an excuse and leave here.* Because unless he killed all four, he would be outgunned. He went along, looking to see if there was any place where he could hide later when the deed was done.

Later in the week, Wayne ronald had changed his plans. He would now kill Michelle, and the daughter, if it came to it. The husband would get the blame, seeing as he had his gun. But he had to get him alone so the plan would work. It was to get the new gun from him and use it on the wife, then plant it and give it back to Sam. The police would find fingerprints on it. He thought, *I could use this other gun, then give it to him and fix the other one so it doesn't work. Then he would think it was the same one.*

The next day, they hunted some more and settled down by the campfire. Wayne ronald eyed the guns; he knew where Sam's was, as he watched earlier as he placed it close to him by a tree. Animals were all around out in the bush, especially wolves. One always had to be prepared. "Well, good night, guys," he said. "I'm gonna get some shut-eye. See you all in the morning."

"Yes," Sam replied, "we should all get some, early rise tomorrow."

Wayne ronald smiled nastily to himself. It was much later that night, just before dawn, that Wayne crept up near the tree, taking the gun and making the switch. *This is a piece of cake*, he thought. He crept back behind the bushes and put the new gun in his knapsack, then went back to sleep.

Come morning, all were awake except Wayne. "Hey!" Sam hollered. Wayne jumped off his bed and swung around and pointed his gun at them. They looked with shock at how fast this man moved, considering they were trained to do just that in the military.

"Sorry, guys," Sam said, "didn't mean to scare you."

Wayne ronald realized he must look like a maniac, pointing the gun. He laughed and replied, "Never holler at a guy when he is sleeping." He smirked. "Especially when he has a gun."

Sam replied with a laugh, "Well, we should know that, I guess." Then he asked, "Were you in military at some time? You move real fast for a local citizen." *Yes*, Wayne thought to himself, *I kill for a living—that's why I'm fast.*

"Yes," he replied, "I was in the army for years since I was seventeen. I trained at a young age." The guys took an instant liking to this man out of respect. He was one of them.

A couple of days later, Michelle went to the shed. *Darn*, she thought, *the light is not working*. She wanted to clean the yard. Sam had taken Lisa into town for supplies for the cabin; now she would have to ask the neighbor for help. She hated to bother him as he pretty much kept to himself, but she didn't want to waste the day away on something trivial. She knocked on the door.

He was watching her coming toward him excitment flowing through his veins as his target was in sight. He raised the rifle and waited it was like hunting, let the target get a little closer. he took aim. Michelle felt something, like lightning, hit her stomach. It was very painful, a sudden thug hard enough to bring her to her knees, losing her breath as she went down. Her eyes focused slightly on a face, now before her, then she lay there in a pool of blood.

Wayne ronald grabbed her lifeless body and hurriedly carried her to the cabin and threw her on the bedroom floor. He then arranged the room to look like someone had come in with the rifle and shot her point-blank. He hurriedly put the rifle by the body and made bloody scuff marks to look like the killer had ran from the room. He then left and closed the door carefully, making sure he left no marks or fingerprints.

Poor Michelle lay there bleeding, but some life was left in this lady; her lively eyes had a flicker in them. Wayne ronald went to the guest house and finished cleaning up the blood by putting leaves and grass and mud on it. He then loaded a pile of leftover sand on there, then he grabbed his hunting gear and the new gun and headed out to the bush. He walked for hours, it seemed. He was all prepared for when the guys found him. He was sure they would look for him as he was in his cabin when Sam left this morning. He then settled on a clearing on the edge of a bank by the river. *If I have to run for it*, he thought, *I can cover my tracks with water*. He had been in a similar situation before. They hunted him down, and he had to swim almost all the way to the other side of an embankment to hide out. But that was a long time ago.

Sam and his daughter Lisa were on their way home. Lisa was laughing about the gift her dad had bought for her mom; it was a little broom decorated with flowers. They said, "Now Mom can sweep and smell the flowers at the same time." Happily they drove along the lane to the cabin. It seemed quiet. Sam happily touched the horn. There was no stir. *That's strange*, he thought. Michelle usually ran out the door to greet him when he did this.

"I wonder where Mom is," Lisa said.

"Maybe the sleepy head can't hear us," he replied.

"Let's just sneak in and surprise her," Lisa said. She loved surprises, as did her mom. They went inside very quietly. Lisa was excited to get there first. She quietly opened the bedroom door. What she saw left her heart cold. Her mother lay on the floor in a pool of blood, and her face was waxen, like a doll's, and her eyes were staring right at Lisa as she opened the door. Lisa screamed and ran toward her father and fell to her knees in shock. Sam grabbed her by the shoulders and let her drag him toward the room. Lisa was vomiting violently now and screaming. Sam ran into the bedroom, and his heart nearly jumped out of his chest. His Michelle lay on the floor, her lips turning blue, so Sam knew he had to get her to the hospital right away. His military training swung into action; he tried getting her to breathe, it did not work he bound her wound up to stop the bleeding as he could see she had lost of blood, time was of the essence now. He calmed Lisa down and called the ambulance to come out; then, mechanically, he called the police. He ran back to his wife's side and laid her head on his lap. There he remained until the police and the ambulance came. Annie rushed into the cabin, sobbing. "Who could have done this horrible thing?" she sobbed over and over. They took Lisa and Annie back into town. Sam didn't want his daughter to stay here one second longer, for he knew they would be looking for a killer.

The whole area was alive with activity now as the police explained to Sam that they had to move fast to get all the clues as to where she was shot. The police didn't tell Sam, but they knew she wasn't shot in the cabin. Not yet, they would tell him later.

Sam was going around as if in a daze. It was only a few hours ago that he had asked Michelle to come along and make a day of going to a movie and having lunch, but she had laughed and replied, "You two go ahead. I'm going to clean the yard and put it in orange bags." Sam looked in the corner. He had brought the little broom and the orange bags for her. He put his head in his hands and sobbed heartbrokenly. His hunting buddies were nearby; they weren't sure what to say or do at this time. Sam looked up all of a sudden, "Hey guys," he said, "let's go check this Wayne's place."

The officer said, "Who else is living around here, Sam?"

"Wayne, one of our hunting buddies," Sam replied.

"Let's go," the officer said, "but let me do my job without interference." They nodded.

They arrived at the guesthouse. There was no sign of the man. Sam opened the door. *Funny*, he thought, *I've been out here lots of times but never in the guesthouse*. The place was empty.

"Maybe he went hunting," Sam said. "There's no sign of his gear." They decided to go look for him. Sam knew where to find Wayne. He thought maybe he went to their campground, but there was no sign of him there. Suddenly they heard a sound. Sam was glad the officer had brought a gun and rifle with him as they didn't. The rifle that shot Michelle had been taken for forensics to examine. Sam suddenly said, "I'm going to the hospital. they agreed.

The police and hunters found Wayne ronald right where he wanted them to. They came up to him quickly; the officer grabbed his book and started questioning him as to his whereabouts this morning. Wayne stood and looked at the group and asked, "What is wrong, guys?"

They told him about Michelle being shot at point-blank range. Wayne mustered his expression as surprise and shock at hearing this. He said, "I'm so sorry to hear that. She is a very nice woman."

The officer said, "We have to ask you a few questions."

Wayne ronald nodded his head in agreement. He told the officer that Michelle had come to his cabin to ask him to fix a light in the shed, and that he said he would come in a little while; but he had a call from his friend in Ontario, so he forgot about the promise. He then decided to go hunting for a while. He was way out in the bush when he heard a gunshot, he said to the officer. He said he didn't make too much of this as it was hunting season up here. The group left shortly after this encounter.

Wayne went on farther in the bush. Just in case his story didn't prove out, he would be ready to get out of there. They would not find him so easily this time. He laughed that graty laugh and was quickly on his way. The guys and police worked their way back to the cabin. The police were now going to search the guesthouse and to look around the yards for clues.

The police had not yet told Sam that his wife was not killed in the cabin, but that she was killed somewhere else and carried there. They wanted to wait and see the results of the rifle as to whom it belonged to. The following few weeks were busy as Sam and his daughter tried to cope with Michelle's injuries. Lisa's twelveth birthday was coming up soon. Sam tried talking her into having a birthday party at home to get her mind off things. Annie was busy taking care of them most days. She also wanted the party to lighten things up and to get life moving again. The next day, they went shopping. Lisa seemed like she was going to cry at any time. Annie also had a hard time holding back tears, as she and Michelle had planned a surprise party for her daughter. They purchased the things they wanted, but when they arrived home, Lisa lost control, and Sam decided to postpone the party for a later date, when michelle got well.

The following week, Sam and Lisa and Annie were having breakfast. There was a knock on the door. Two police officers stood there. "Morning, Officers," Sam greeted them, they replied good morning sam.

They looked at each other and glanced around. "We have come to place you under arrest, Sam, for the attempted murder of your wife, Michelle."

Sam turned very pale as he replied, "There must be some mistake, guys. I love my wife! Why would I want to hurt her?"

They replied, "The rifle forensics test has proven that the rifle belongs to one Samuel Reid. Plus, there were your fingerprints on there." The officer looked at Sam. "It's your gun, Sam."

Lisa was listening to all of this. "No no no!" she screamed. "My dad didn't shoot my mom! You are making a mistake!" Sam tried to calm her down and called Annie to come get Lisa, from the kitchen.

"My god!" She cried. "What is happening to this family?" They took Sam away in handcuffs. A sobbing Lisa was holding on to his hands. They had to pull her from her dad. Sam's eyes filled with tears.

"I will be back," he said. "This is a mistake, Lisa. Daddy will be back."

They put Sam in prison after a picture-taking session and finger printing. Sam was afraid of what was going to happen to his daughter and wife, for he knew he was innocent. The police kept on checking at Sam's insistence as to the gun. He told them of someone stealing his old rifle, and that he had bought a new one. They looked into this in the following weeks and Sam was out on bail until his trial. They were hoping he was right as they liked this man and he had no killer instinct in him.

In a little town like this, everyone knew each other, and they had known Sam and Michelle for years, but right now all the evidence pointed to Sam.

It was early in November when things came to a head. The police came to Sam's home for a chat. They asked Sam for his gun and wanted to know when and where Sam's other gear was before it was stolen. Sam took them to the shed, and they dusted for fingerprints. The whole shed was examined by the police. A few days later, Sam got the news that all charges against him were dropped as they found different prints on some of the old clothes that was in the shed, for this person had gone through some other stuff, as well as stealing the hunting gear. The officers did not want to tell Sam on the phone, so the next day they came to his home while Lisa was at school.

"Sam," they said, "we have a lot to tell you." Sam had coffee made and invited them inside. "First of all, Sam, we have evidence that your wife was not shot in the cabin."

Attentively Sam listened in a daze as they told him the gruesome details about his wife. They had gotten in contact with the Ontario police department, and they had matched fingerprints to one Wayne ronald clum.

"That's our hunting buddy!" Sam gasped. The police officer held up his hand. They also had discovered that Wayne ronald clum was a contract killer, and a few years back he was contracted to kill Michelle's mother, Beth.

"Oh my god!" Sam exclaimed.

"There is more," the officer replied. "He has made a mistake, and had mistaken Michelle for her mother all these years, for they look almost exactly alike. He came here to kill your wife, Sam, and he almost succeeded this time."

Sam jumped off the chair. "Well, let's go get this killer!"

"It's not that simple, Sam," the officer said. "We have to set him up somehow, or else he will run. We are hoping he doesn't hear any news." Sam was very angry and frustrated. He was kind of angry at himself for not looking into this guy's background when he came to rent the guest house, like he was trained to do on occasions. "Then what are you waiting for!" he exclaimed. "I know where he is as we speak."

The next morning the troops set out for the manhunt. The snow was falling softly now as the winter was here. The trees looked lovely in their shrouded blanket of white. It was a soft, mild kind of morning. The police officers were glad of the snow as they knew it would be easier to catch the killer.

Wayne ronald clum was sitting, having his morning coffee. Admiring the white beauty around him, he thought one of the bushes looked like a white lump of sugar. As he looked closer, he saw that it was a rabbit. "Oh boy." he smirked. "I can have lunch today."

He opened the knife case and threw the knife with precision. The rabbit lay there, bleeding. Wayne covered it with snow so as to keep it good until he could build a fire. Farther down the river, he thought how happy he was to finally get this job done. He smirked nastily now. *If I had some way to hear the news to see if the husband is in jail, then there would be no hurry to leave this place.* He liked the idea of being alone in the bush. There was some kind of comforting feeling with it all being so serene. He thought, *I'll build a cabin here one day and live by myself in the bush.* He could still take calls for his work,—which, by the way, he had no contact with his people lately other than the next job. He took out his phone from the gear bag and opened it. He started dialing the numbers.

Not too far away, the police stopped in their tracks. "Listen," one said, "it's a signal." They had rigged up a signal for any sound of phones or radios and mobile phones on their machines. Sam was very excited. "That may be him," he said.

"Well, it sure could be." replied the officers.

They followed the signal for some miles, then all of a sudden it stopped. The troops were puzzled as it now was getting closer to them. They drew out their guns, ready for anything. Sam thought, *This guy may come out with guns blazing.*

It got closer but it stopped. The police got their speakers out. "Wayne ronald clum, you are under arrest for the murder of Michelle Reid." There was no sound. Suddenly out of the bush came a moose. It charged between them; it was in a panic as the beeping was coming from it. This guy had rigged his phone on this animal by injuring it in the leg to bring it down so he could do this thing. Sam realized that this man was very smart and trained from somewhere, but he found out earlier from the police that he was not a military person. Whoever he worked for trained him in survival techniques.

Wayne ronald, meanwhile, picked up on the speakers. Even from the distance, he was. He ran farther into the rugged bush. Up there, you had to know where you were going. Wayne ronald did not. He ran for his life now. The snow was leaving tracks; he somehow had to cover them. He cut off some bough and dragged it behind him as he ran. He looked back, and it was working. Little did he realize that the marks were now there for the hunters and police to follow. *I must get back to the river*, Wayne thought. He smirked to himself, *They won't get me there.* He finally reached a river some ten miles away from the hunt. He swam toward the other side. The current was very strong, and it was so cold that he started to go under. Just to stay afloat, He grabbed a tree branch hanging on the river's edge. He pulled himself out. He was now freezing, for it had turned cold as the day went into evening. He dared not light a fire, so he pulled out his old blankets that he had stolen from the shed and shivering now, and wrapped himself with it to warm up, listening all the time for any sound.

The troops and hunters decided to set up camp for the night as it was cold and getting dark. They lit a fire and prepared a meal, then each took turns to watch for animals or maybe the killer coming their way. And that was exactly what Wayne ronald planned to do in the night. He got ready to backtrack. That way, they would be running on a fool's chase. He laughed to himself. *Maybe I can get more targets—those officers will not know what hit them.*

It was now snowing a little heavier, than before. Sam thought to himself, *Winter is here, and soon Christmas.* He got misty-eyed thinking of his Michelle who loved this season but she was safe now, so he had joined the hunt. He had offered to take first watch. The officers agreed only because he was trained in the military. It was a beautiful night with the snow coming down in fat flakes, and the silence was deafening. Sam gazed around. The tall trees were a blanket of white, and the river was calm and quiet.

He thought he heard something around the trees. He checked it out; it was only a rabbit. Later, toward dawn, he heard it again. It sounded like rustling of leaves in the bush area. Probably some small animal. But he did not know that it was Wayne ronald creeping by the camp on his way to a better hiding place.

Morning came and Sam went to sleep for a while as the troops were all on the move. They had meals, and then some of them stayed with Sam while others scouted around for clues as to the whereabouts of Wayne. They came back sometime later to report that they had found a campsite some ways back, about ten miles with marks in the snow and found out he was trying to hide his footsteps. They followed the branch marks to the river downstream, but then it ended. Wayne ronald came to the end of a road that he thought led to the cabins, but it led to an old mining site. *This is even better*, he thought. *They will never find me here.* He went past the warning signs and hunkered down underground in a space that he assumed was an old lunchroom.

There was an old bench on tattered legs, and an old table of sorts. He looked around more as he had lit an oil lamp that he found in the shed that day. He snickered that Sam was well-prepared when he went hunting. It was a dismal place, thought Wayne. The miners must have been not happy working here as the smell alone would make it hard for them to work in, for it was uranium mining that was done there. *Well,* he thought, *I have been in worse places in my lifetime.*

The troops were on the way again. They had no idea where to look now as the trail they found had ended. Sam said, "Let's check the river, maybe he came out a little farther down and said for sure he swam to the other side."

After hours of looking for clues as to where he might be, they went back to camp for supper. After some time, they were discussing getting a guide to lead them. There was a guide who lived here all his life and knew the North backcountry. They got on the two-way radio and called the department and made a plan to meet the guide. But the guide said he would find them. Much later that evening, they heard a noise coming toward their campsite. Rifles ready, they waited for it to come out of the bush, but it was the guide. He was a very tall man with a pleasant smile.

"Hi," he said. "I'm your guide. I know this country very well. We will find this man, for he had been filled in on it all." He was an expert tracker.

He said, "We will backtrack all the trails you have been on. I need to examine it all in the morning." They agreed as this man seemed to know his job very well. Next day found everybody up and on the go again. It had snowed all night, and it was getting colder. They were dressed warmly, but it was now miserable as the cold winds had come up. They looked around for the guide, but there was no sign of him. Sam said maybe he went scouting around. Just then he came back.

"I found tracks here this morning just before dawn," said the guide. This man has sent you on a goose chase. He has backtracked toward town." They looked at him in surprise.

"I did not see anything," said Sam. "But I heard an animal nearby in the bush last night."

"That was no animal, my friend," replied the guide. "That was the man whom you seek. He passed by your camp just before dawn this morning."

"We better get moving. If he reaches town, he will be gone out of range," the officers said. They quickly packed their gear and headed toward the cabin, where their vehicles were with the guide in the lead.

The going was long and rough and very cold. As the winds blew snow all around them, it became hard to see in this weather. The guide kept a steady pace as all tried to keep warm.

Wayne ronald was getting cold now as it was already damp and cold underground. He walked out to check on the weather, and the storm met him face on. He shivered as his clothes were still damp from the river. He thought about taking a chance and lighting a fire in there, but how it would go, he was not sure. *There may be gasses in here*, he thought. *I have to do something.* He looked around the area. It looked like wonderland with all the snow. The winds had come up also, which made it a little difficult to light a fire, but he had to do something. He found an old tin can by the entrance and lit a small fire in the can and placed it just inside of the opening of the mine. He warmed his hands, now shivering badly. *I have to get out of here*, he thought. *They may be far from here. This is my chance.* He was going to stay there, but it got too cold even for him. He went back inside, grabbed his belongings and rifle, and set out toward town. *I should be* there *and on a bus by night fall*, he figured.

The swirling snow was blinding. There were whiteouts all around the police and hunters, They finally made it to the cabins. Some of them went to the guesthouse and some to Annies cabin, thankful they had somewhere to stay, for now this was a blinding snowstorm, one of the worst so far.

As he walked toward town, Wayne ronald clum could not see where he was going, but he kept moving in this blinding white storm. It had gotten worse over the past few minutes.

The troops and guide were thinking the same thing. "We will stay at the cabins tonight," Sam said. "They are closer than town." They all agreed as a person could not see anything in this storm. They settled in for the night. The guide went outside to look around and see if anything was amiss. He was used to this weather; he could see things that others would not see. Wayne Ronald

Was getting colder by the minute. *I must get in somewhere*, he thought. The cabins were around here somewhere. *If I could find them, I will be safe*. He looked into the distance but could see nothing. He fell to the ground, not wanting to get up now as he felt warm lying there, but he knew he would die if he did not move. He got up and staggered toward where he thought the cabins would be, but there was nothing but white swirls of snow and wind. He went onward hoping for any shelter now as he was feeling very, very cold and tired.

Suddenly he saw lights. *Am I dreaming?* he thought. *These are the cabins, but there is someone in there*. He looked toward the guesthouse. That also was alight. *I've got to get out of here*, Wayne thought. *I have walked into their arms*. He staggered across to the other side. *I will hole up in the shed for tonight*, he thought. Slowly he crept into the shed. The lock was not working since he had robbed the place. *They are so close now*, he thought. At first light he would have to make tracks again, but for now he snuggled under some old clothes that lay in a box and went to sleep with his rifle in hand.

This storm had raged on through the night. Everyone was thrown offtrack, and they had no idea that the murderer was only a few feet away. The early dawn saw Wayne ronald up and creeping away into the bush, as the storm was over but very cold and slippery still. He knew any minute he would be caught. He walked and ran through the bush toward town. His truck had given out on him a few weeks ago, so he had to make it by foot. The town was at least three miles away. But if he ran a little, it would be quicker, and he would keep warmer. Suddenly he came upon an old car parked by the side of an old barn. *Well,* he smirked, *things are picking up*. He jumped into the car for it was not locked and played with the ignition wires and got it going. He sped out of there in a fast pace toward town. He happened to glance back, and in the rearview mirror he could see a man shouting and making gestures toward him in an angry manner. "Sorry, old boy." He laughed out loud. "You will get this back someday."

He turned on the radio and heard his name and all the details. They had been looking for him for days. "Not anymore." He laughed. "I am going to fix it so no one will arrest me. They will go down or I will." He laughed like a crazy man as he picked up speed. The roads were icy due to the snow, and he slid blindly all over the road.

The troops were all ready for another try at finding this killer. Suddenly the mobile rang. An officer answered. It was a man complaining about his car being stolen about two hours ago. The police wanted all the details, but the man had not seen the driver, only as he drove away. They got excited.

Sam said, "I bet that's our man."

The guide came in just then and said, "This man was very close. Last night he was in the shed. I found this." He handed a knife to the officer.

"That's my knife!" Sam exclaimed. "It was stolen along with all of my other hunting gear." The officer put it in a plastic bag.

"Yes, that's our man, and he is in a vehicle, which means we are wasting time out here." They quickly got on all police radios and put out a call to get this guy. Sam thought of his wife and was glad that she was safe in the hospital for they had announced her death on the news cast so the killer would not go after her again.

An inspector was in control of the investigation. He had Michelle pronounced dead on arrival at the hospital. He knew the killer was still at large; they kept a strict eye on who came to visit. And it would be some time before Michelle would be well again. Wayne ronald clum thought he had killed this woman, and that was the way they announced it on the news—that she was dead.

Wayne ronald had a hard time keeping the vehicle on the highway as it was getting more slippery as he drove very fast. *Got to get out of this place*, he thought. *I need the big city to get lost in. Well,* he smirked with satisfaction, *at least the job is finished here.*

All of a sudden he came upon an animal in the middle of the road. It was a large moose. It stood there as if transfixed by the car lights. Wayne swerved to avoid hitting it as he would not survive the hit of a big animal in the small car. And in doing so, the vehicle went out of control and crashed through a broken guardrail made of wood. He plummeted at least forty feet down the ravine. The vehicle spun over and over 'til it burst into flames. The gas tank was hit several times by rocks on the way down, and ignited the gas. Wayne Ronald clum would not be going anywhere, anymore as he was dead.

The troops hurried as much as they could to get to town. The roads were very icy. Suddenly they slowed to a stop, for the guide had spotted something down below as the flames were still burning very high. They later identified the badly burned body as Wayne Ronald Clum. They had to get a helicopter to fly down the ravine to identify the body. It was finally over for Michelle. After a few weeks, the case was at last closed as there was no family to report this to. Michelle was improving a little every day. She would never forget that face or what happened to her. But as she says, "I'm alive with a family that loves me, and that is all that matters." Her little home by the brook is more special now as they are all happy together. The birds are singing, and the little brook is gurgling. As much to say—all is well that ends well, and she knows that her mother is looking down on this family and smiling.

The End

Edwards Brothers,Inc!
Thorofare, NJ 08086
28 June, 2010
BA2010179